body language

Previous Winners of the Katherine Anne Porter Prize
in Short Fiction
Barbara Rodman, series editor

The Stuntman's Daughter by Alice Blanchard
Rick DeMarinis, Judge

Here Comes the Roar by Dave Shaw
Marly Swick, Judge

Let's Do by Rebecca Meacham
Jonis Agee, Judge

What Are You Afraid Of? by Michael Hyde
Sharon Oard Warner, Judge

Body
Language

BY KELLY MAGEE

2006 WINNER, KATHERINE ANNE PORTER PRIZE IN SHORT FICTION

University of North Texas Press
Denton, Texas

10 9 8 7 6 5 4 3 2 1

Permissions:
University of North Texas Press
P.O. Box 311336
Denton, TX 76203-1336

The paper used in this book meets the minimum requirements of the American National Standard for Permanence of Paper for Printed Library Materials, z39.48.1984. Binding materials have been chosen for durability.

Library of Congress Cataloging-in-Publication Data

Magee, Kelly, 1976-
  Body language / by Kelly Magee.
    p. cm. — (Katherine Anne Porter Prize in Short Fiction series ; no. 5)
  ISBN-13: 978-1-57441-219-2 (pbk. : alk. paper)
  ISBN-10: 1-57441-219-1 (pbk. : alk. paper)
  1. Gender identity—Fiction. 2. Lesbians—Fiction. 3. Southern States—Social life and customs—Fiction. I. Title.
  PS3613.A3428B63 2006
  813'.6—dc22
                              2006022580

Body Language is Number 5 in the Katherine Anne Porter Prize in Short Fiction Series

Text design by Carol Sawyer/Rose Design

For my family
And especially, for Lauren

contents

acknowledgments

Thanks to the editors of the following journals and anthologies in which these stories first appeared, some in different format: *Colorado Review*: "Body Language"; *Crab Orchard Review*: "As Human As You Are Standing Here"; *The Cream City Review*: "Heat Rises"; *Folio*: "Fortune"; *Indiana Review* (with special thanks to Danit Brown): "All the America You Want"; *Quarterly West* and *The 2004 Robert Olen Butler Prize Stories*: "Not People, Not This"; *Marlboro Review*: "The Business of Souls"; *Ohio Writer*: a portion of "Straitjacket" called "COTA Bus Driver #18"; *Tartts: Incisive Fiction from Emerging Writers*: "Vertical Miles."

Thanks to the Money for Women/Barbara Deming Memorial Fund, Inc., for their financial help and moral support.

Thanks to Dan Chaon and Barbara Rodman for their encouragement, and to Karen DeVinney and everyone at the University of North Texas Press for their hard work in the publication of this book.

Special thanks to Lee K. Abbott, Dorothy Allison, Michelle Herman, Erin McGraw, Lee Martin, and Valerie Miner for their guidance with these stories, and general wisdom about writing; to Mollie Blackburn and Mindi Rhoades for their support and friendship; to fellow writers Katie Pierce, Mike Kardos, Teline Guerra, Erica Beeney, Keith Cooper, Jeff Butler, and Chris Coake for their help on many drafts of these stories; to my family, my parents, Joy Langone and Tim Magee, my sisters, Cassie Quest and Erin Magee, and extended family Andrew Langone and Al and Terry Kenney, for being the wonderful people you are; and to Lauren Kenney, for everything.

not people, not this

In many rural areas, there is nothing for a tornado to hit, nor anyone to see it.

—*The Handy Weather Answer Book*

In Alabama, a tornado touches down.

Within minutes, things begin to change. Tiny green tomatoes ripen instantly. Chickens lose their feathers. Whole cotton fields spoil; their curled leaves smell like rust. The blotch on the TV map turns blue to red in three counties. Cars scatter like grass clippings.

A woman in Montgomery opens her cupboard to find every dish cracked in thirds. A man in Mobile gets up from his recliner just as it bursts its seams, spews white stuffing into the living room. People all over the state report prank phone calls—hang-ups. Alarms engage for no reason.

Grocery stores in Birmingham sell out of raw hamburger, veal, steak. People growl. Animals murmur. The wind blows grills down the street, still lit, still smoking.

Here, storms make us believe things we never would on a sunny day. We'll accept weather as a defense for almost any crime. Like insanity, you can plead thunderstorm. Full moon. Tornado. We'll believe the lightning made you do it. That the clerk lost the money in the register. The wife just up and disappeared.

It could happen.

When the sirens went off in Montgomery, Opelika, a forty-minute drive away, had already lost power. Residents emptied the main streets, and the parking lots of Kroger and Super Wal-Mart. Those who had basements retreated to them with flashlights and radios. WKKR reported the tornado to be somewhere in the country, headed directly for town.

In the lightless Drunken Dime, two men listened to the weather report and toasted themselves with whiskey. They'd known each other from birth, but they were not friends. They were men, alive at the same time, who exchanged money and nods in the bar. One, Trooper, owned the place. The other, Ames, had been on his way out when the bar went dark, but knew an opportunity for free booze when he saw one. He'd suggested a last toast to the storm, and since their fathers had been neighbors as boys and their mothers still held bridge parties together—and because, in a way, they were of the same stock—Trooper had agreed. Really, he wanted to be home, ushering his daughter and wife, who'd called the bar three times, into the basement, pulling a mattress over their heads. His own father had tied the family dogs down by their feet, but Trooper wasn't a violent man. Not anymore. He would pack the dogs away in kennels, let them howl and chew on the wire as they always did when the wind picked up.

The men toasted themselves first, then the weather. On the radio, the tornado played like a slow-motion football game: yards lost and gained.

The second shot went down like bad blood. The sun hadn't quite set—in summer the daylight outlasted the day—and the bar was light enough for Ames to notice Trooper eyeing him. Ames knew that Trooper wouldn't make him pay for the drinks if he caused a fuss. Trooper knew that Ames didn't mind screwing his friends over once in a while, and they weren't even friends.

"There's nothing like a hard drink in the dark," Ames said. He worked at a pawn shop, but might've owned a bar himself, had he gotten his act together in high school. He'd flunked out because he couldn't keep his hands out of trouble. He had a thing for the sucker punch. Everything made him mad, but especially girls: the way they flipped their hair like it didn't drive him crazy. And then, twice he'd gotten caught unzipped in indecent places. Jerking off in the cafeteria bathroom, and a closet in the life science class. The principal had made sure Ames failed four out of seven classes, the requisite amount. He'd left in tenth grade, applied for a job at the pawn shop where he could pocket a little cash on the side without the owner ever knowing.

Trooper raised his empty glass. Paused for tact. "Guess you'll be heading home now," he said.

Ames held his glass in front of his eye. Trooper's face swam.

"Real nice," he said. "Really, man. Real goddamn nice." He turned the glass on its side, aimed it like a dart at Trooper's face. The nasal voice on WKKR warned anyone on the road to seek shelter.

"What's nice?" Trooper said.

"You're going to send me out in this." Ames aimed. Leveled. Aimed again. "Aren't you?"

"Yeah," Trooper said. "I am."

Ames threw the glass, but not at Trooper. He smashed it on the floor. These days, he was given to fits of rage that didn't amount to much. He wasn't really dangerous—not to Trooper, anyway. He had the social skills of a mosquito. He wanted to be a better man, but didn't quite know how to go about it.

"One drink," Trooper said. "You said one drink. We've had two. Let's go." He was bigger, so he hauled Ames into the parking lot by his collar. It wasn't that he didn't feel sorry for the guy. Trooper understood Ames maybe more than anyone else. His wife said it was because of their proximity as babies. Really, it was because they both dealt with fear the same way: they hit. When he got married, Trooper had developed a technique for disarming his fists: one finger at a time, five counts in between. He was aware how close he'd been to becoming an Ames. But now he had other worries. He had the wife and kid. He had priorities.

Ames, on the other hand, lived alone in a trailer that stunk of gas leaking from the stove. Neither the stove nor the trailer would have a chance in a tornado. If he went home, he'd be surfing the roof in an hour. He'd be heading scalp-first for the nearest tree.

"Go home," Trooper said, and Ames thought, *Easy for you.*

"I'm going," Ames said, shrugging his coat back into place. Trooper revved the motor on his pickup and backed it onto the road, kicking up gravel dust. Ames toed one of the larger stones in the lot. He dislodged it, tossed it into the air. The wind was picking up. He had nowhere to go. Two years ago, a storm had flattened half his trailer park, and ever since he'd tried to find other kinds of shelter. But he'd run aground. He'd gotten kicked out of libraries, state buildings, even churches. He had a temper. He couldn't help himself.

On the third toss, the wind pushed the rock forward in the air, and Ames had to run to catch it. That was the last thing Trooper saw in his rearview: Ames hurrying across the parking lot to catch a rock that, just then, seemed light as a bubble. Behind him, miles of abandoned fields—the Drunken Dime's backyard. In front, the sky, still blue.

In Birmingham, weather was nothing if not conversation. Three out of every five families were on the phone. Grandmothers called grandkids up north—they worried. Parents called dorms in Auburn and Tuscaloosa, told their new college students to go to the lobby. People tuned their TVs to the Weather Channel, then dialed up somebody to tell about The Time. The Time crazy uncle so-and-so went outside in red flannel p.j.s to videotape a twister. The Time a cow turned up at the intersection of Thatch and King, miles from any farm, alive and mooing under the traffic light. Pencils through trees and trees through houses. Strip malls turned on end. Near misses. Almosts. Danger that made their knees weak from two hundred miles away.

"Obsessing about weather is a Southern thing, isn't it?" our friends in the North say. And it's true: down here, we're tied as much to climate as to place. We're up to our necks in it. But this is not geography, we tell them. This is realism. This is eight hundred confirmed touch downs, this is ten thousand deaths this century. This is deviant meteorology. That's why the whole state pays attention. That's what we mean when—surveying the wreckage, giving a statement to the news—we say we've been saved.

We're not kidding ourselves. The sky, like God or Santa Claus, knows when we're asleep.

"The sky is watching," our mothers warned us before bed. "Say your prayers and go to sleep fast."

May called Judy, her neighbor, at five till eight. It took three tries to get someone to pick up.

"We were down in the basement," Judy's husband said.

"I just wanted to check in," May said, and her voice sounded older to herself. She always felt elderly when she was checking in. And she wasn't elderly. Not yet, anyway. "I'm leaving now for Saving Grace."

"Why don't you come over," Judy's husband said. "It's closer."

"I don't mind the walk," May said. Children were yelling in the background, and the thought of weathering a storm with a seven- and nine-year-old made her head ache. The children were fine, *children* were fine, but May preferred the company of tamer species—the dogs she kept in her house that'd just had puppies. They were rescues, coaxed into her car from the side of a country road. She'd had one little girl, long ago, whom she didn't speak to anymore. Her daughter, thirty-two now, lived out West. She'd left for college in Arizona and returned queer. Literally. She'd come home talking about how flat Alabama seemed, how green, and by the way, mom, I'm in love with a woman. They didn't keep in touch. At times, May missed her. Especially in heavy weather. She'd checked the train schedule twice in the past year. She didn't fly. Pretty soon, she'd be too old to travel at all.

"Anyway," May said, "I've got plenty of time. It's not even dark yet."

"Okay," Judy's husband said. "But be careful."

"Of course," May said.

She made a bed of towels in her bathtub and, one by one, transferred the litter of puppies into it. They were just opening their eyes. She kissed their wet noses.

"Good luck," she said as she shut the door. She knew people who loved pets like babies, but she was practical. She loved them like animals, which wasn't more or less, just different. And like animals, they had to fend for themselves. She, on the other hand, needed the help of the Saving Grace church, where the walls were sturdy and volunteers helped steady her nerves. She'd gone there for years. She knew when to leave her house by the way the clouds started to churn. She gathered her rain slicker and boots, her flashlight. She looked forward to the walk— twenty minutes of open air before being cooped up in the church basement. A few more minutes of peace while the squall surged forth behind her.

Judy called just as May was walking out the door. They had something of a psychic bond, the two of them. May had rescued Judy, too, several times. They were so close that they often guessed each other's thoughts.

"Let us drive you, May," Judy said. "Please."

"You know I like to walk." May surveyed the sky, glanced at the clock over the kitchen stove.

"It'll take me five minutes to get the kids settled down, and I'll take you myself."

"Really," May said. "Don't worry."

In five minutes May would be halfway down the road, thinking of the puppies in her bathtub. She'd be rounding the corner where the hardware store was, halfway to Kmart, then the Drunken Dime. She'd cut through fields of asparagus and sorghum, and by the time Judy had coaxed the kids back into the basement, May would be knee deep in greenery. Soft clay staining the soles of her shoes. Then she'd cut through the Tractor Graveyard, a dumping ground for old balers, rotary plows, harvesters, and threshers. There was a crop duster from 1942 back there, and a windmill. No one could say for sure where the windmill was from. After the

Tractor Graveyard, May would finally arrive at the rear entrance of the church.

"I'm worried about her," Judy told her husband after hanging up. She looked once out the window, but May wasn't there. "Something about this isn't right."

That's all there is. A bar confrontation, two phone calls. The evidence is hard to piece together—the tornado got most of it. There are missing person reports and police records and a bit of investigative work, but nothing that adds up to much. Only the stories, and those have grown harder to find. In Opelika, we're always telling each other's stories, but you have to know when to pay attention. How to find the facts in the muck. You have to be clever about asking questions, and you have look away at the right moment. Nobody likes to think they're a gossip.

The tornado touched down, and it changed things. Afterward, May came up missing. Ames's car was still parked outside the Drunken Dime, and one window in the bar was broken. Trooper found a rock on the bar floor. Judy broke into May's house when she didn't get a return phone call, and found the dogs whimpering in the bathroom. Ames didn't come to work for a week, and when he finally turned up, his story kept changing. He'd gotten sick of his life and had headed south. He'd taken the bus to Montgomery the morning after the tornado. He'd hitchhiked. He'd stayed with friends he couldn't name.

A bar confrontation, two phone calls. Everything else, the sky sucked up.

When asked about May, Ames first said, "Never heard of her."

As for May, popular belief was that she'd been redeemed, taken body and soul into the bosom of heaven. It'd happened to several of the town's great-grandmothers. Some people said Ames had killed her in a rage and used the storm to cover up his crime. The police said the two cases weren't related, and they warned reporters about unduly frightening the public.

"Nobody killed anybody," Officer Gary Scott said. "There's no evidence that even puts these two in the same place."

Still others suggested May might've gone to see the forsaken daughter. Judy, who could guess May's thoughts, kept quiet. Efforts to contact the daughter were unsuccessful.

Of all the stories about weather, this one's our favorite. In 1986, a tornado decimated the Saving Grace Baptist Church. For two years, the congregation held Sunday services in the high school cafeteria, pooling money and prayers. When they finished the new church, it was the biggest for miles around. Stadium seating, hundred-foot plate glass windows, video screens on either side of the pulpit. Electronic hymnals. The whole shebang. Visible at night from the highway by the security lights shining above it.

In honor of the new structure, the members changed the name from Saving Grace to Resurrection.

In 1991, on a sticky night in June, a tornado demolished the whole heavenly thing.

Not to be deterred and thinking brave thoughts of Job, the congregation returned to the high school and prayed. They held bake sales by the hundreds, donated life savings. Teenagers washed cars until their fingers ached. The Baptist Coalition and the City Council pitched in. Soon, on the flattened remains of two previous churches, the third church arose. This one had moving sidewalks, a weight room, a chlorinated fountain for baptisms. They named it Perseverance of Saints. They were the saints. They hung a wall-sized, bronze plaque on the front that said, A Mighty Fortress Is Our God.

Of course, it was doomed.

When, in 1998, the Perseverance succumbed to a double whammy of two successive tornadoes in the same day, the town gave up. Half its citizens converted to Presbyterianism. Two years later, a contractor was brave enough to build an open-air mall on the site, and no tornado has hit it. Yet.

It's all true. The sky is watching.

One story says this.

As a kid, Ames's mother's friends had complained about him, said he stared at them too much. Said he had raven eyes. He'd had trouble with women all his life, he didn't dispute that. In adulthood, he'd turned to phone lines. Sex lines. He missed the flesh and blood quality of peeping, sure. Growing up, he'd liked to watch the spaces women occupied, the way rooms moved around them. He'd been your average boy with binoculars until high school. He started with phone lines after tenth grade, when he didn't have much access to real women any more.

He'd gotten out of control, of late. He'd been having trouble getting it up, and sometimes he paid for four or five calls a night, for nothing. Just to hold his sad, tired dick in his hand and listen to a woman talk. Then, two weeks ago, a girl had hyperventilated right into the receiver. At first, Ames had thought—you know. Part of the act. But no. She'd gotten worse. Wouldn't stop, wouldn't hang up. She made Ames so angry he'd ripped the magazine he was holding.

"Get off the goddamn phone," he'd said.

He tried to hang up and dial again, but she was still there.

"I'm paying for this," he said. "Get a fucking paper bag."

Breath. Breathbreath.

"Hang it up. Now."

Breath.

He'd yelled at her, bent over his legs and *yelled*. Found himself growing hard, his hand working below. He put the phone on his leg where he could hear her infuriating wheezing. He leaned back and groaned. His fingers grew slick.

Turned out it was the best thing she could've done.

That was what made him nervous: he'd gotten off on his own anger. It worried him. He'd begun to have violent fantasies. Twisting limbs, pushing in throats with his thumb. Gaspings. Stranglings. He didn't know what to make of it. He vowed to become better. He knew most people thought of him as a Class A pervert, but really, even he had his limits.

One Iola Jennings of Huntsville, former Call Center Operator, will verify parts of this story. "I just froze up," she says. "I couldn't move, I could barely breathe. It was my first time, you know, doing that sort of thing. I thought it would be easy. But this guy—he was just too creepy. I could hear it in his voice. The creepiness. He got off on it, for sure. I'm not in that line of work anymore."

The crime scene, had there been one, might've looked like this: a bar with a busted window, a ratty brown car, gravel pushed outward at a point cater-corner to the door, as if in struggle. But as it was, no scene, no crime. The tornado inhaled it all: evidence, indignity. The redemption story took off like wildfire. We do this: tell stories. We imagine May was lifted out of the mire. We're not exactly covering up the truth, so much as softening the blow to our souls. We blame weather. We make it so we can watch the news wide-eyed, virginal. People are not capable of this. Not people. Not this.

Montgomery, AL. A row of pine trees on West Magnolia Street has lost its bark, reports homeowner Edward Greathouse.

After the tornado Tuesday evening, Greathouse and three of his neighbors found their trees stripped of all bark. Otherwise, the trees are intact. All vegetation surrounding the trees, including flowers planted underneath, remain unharmed.

"I mean, there's not one broken branch," Greathouse said. "Just these trees, naked as new babies."

Greathouse says he knows of no scientific explanation for the phenomenon. He is not religious, but says he does believe in miracles.

"I believe this was a sign," he said. "We've been personally blessed." He was unclear, however, on the exact meaning of the blessing.

The trees were each over fifty years old.

Alexander City, AL. In a small town in rural Alabama, a Fowl Processing Plant was damaged by an F4 tornado yesterday. An F4 is one of the most violent tornadoes, and can stay on the ground for an hour or more. The plant had been vacated, and there were no reported injuries.

One resident of Alexander City, Jim Curtis, claims the destruction began to happen minutes *before* the tornado hit. Curtis blames the animals themselves—hundreds of caged Cornish Rock broiler chickens—for staging a jail break just prior to the tornado.

"Those chickens started fussing a full thirty minutes before the tornado hit," Curtis said. "I swear it. I heard their squawking from a block away."

Another source, who wished to remain anonymous, confirms Curtis's account. According to this source, the chickens spontaneously revolted, breaking free of their cages and wandering out onto State Road 22. The tornado hit approximately ten minutes later. The freed chickens were later found in neighbors' yards and

SR-22 was closed for several hours while police tried to round the chickens up.

"You've never seen anything like it," the source stated.

When asked why the chickens might want to escape, the source replied, "I don't know. I guess maybe they knew what was coming for them. Animals can be perceptive that way."

Dozens of the animals were injured or killed by traffic before the police arrived. Of the remaining live chickens, forty-two are still unaccounted for.

May's wrist was thin. Ames admired it at first. He thought it looked flexible, bendy like a straw. May could feel the tornado in the ground before it ever came near. Her wrist was not nearly as flexible as Ames thought.

We called him Uncle. We never knew his real name. He wasn't anyone's uncle, just a neighbor a few houses down. As a young man, he'd grown potatoes that were the consistency of sugar—grainy. As an old man, he sold his farm to a white corn company and moved into a trailer. He was the only person we ever knew to survive a lightning strike and a tornado both. The lightning made him mean. The tornado cured him.

People said he'd been a good man, but after he got struck, we knew not to go near him. He assaulted kids; he molested them. Later we'd call these Ames Problems, but that wasn't entirely fair. Ames never hurt a kid, not that we knew of. Uncle sat in a folding chair in his front yard for years, until he got his legs back. We never saw him go inside. His wife brought food to him. She said he wouldn't eat anything but white corn. We could get close enough to flick his ears if we crept up from behind, and he'd reach out with his cane and try to smack our legs as we ran away. We knew better than to get caught. If you got caught, you were doomed. You'd return home with bruises, maybe a bit rumpled in the pants. Our parents told us not to go near him. We couldn't stay away.

He drove his wife from him with that cane when the tornado came. Told her he wanted to meet it face to ugly face. The police found him in a ditch.

"I wrestled that tornado," he said. "The tornado lost."

He was dizzy for weeks, but when he could finally stop his eyes from rolling, he was good again. He didn't beat anyone with the cane.

Dinah Beaman tells this story. "I'm going back," she said to her first husband, six months before they were divorced. They were living in Ohio. Dinah, like many of us, had moved away, moved back, moved away. There was something about the South she could never quite leave. She kept wanting to return to her roots, the clean, white stalks of them. But when she got there, all she ever found was kudzu. "It's just for a visit," she told her husband. "To see if something grabs me."

"In Opelika," her husband said, "something's bound to."

At seven-fifteen in Opelika, the Watch became a Warning.

Sitting in his car outside the Drunken Dime, Ames thought about being good. He was waiting for the tornado. His only chance was averting it in his car. If he could see the thing, he could beat it. He'd tried to get back into the bar, had smashed the front window with a rock, but his arm wasn't long enough to unlock the door, even if he climbed on top of a parking meter. The last tornado to hit Opelika had thundered by and taken half of his neighbors with it. He'd spent the entire time crouched in his shower with couch cushions clutched to his head, saying, "Oh shit, oh no, no," and pissing on himself. He was not a brave man.

The experience had fucked him up royally, and he wasn't about to go through it again. He'd started having dreams about tornadoes giving him blow jobs. He'd had about all he could take.

That was his thought before he saw the woman: *a better man.* Then he saw her, and the tornado touched down, and things changed. The wind whipped her hair into spikes, plastered her windbreaker to her chest. He knew her, faintly, like he knew everyone. She was alone. She was thin and strong. Once, before he'd been ruined by bullying fathers and bartenders, he might've married a woman like this, been a gentle man. He could see himself, arm linked with hers, pressing foreheads to the wind. Somewhere between that vision and his slumped position in the car was where his life had gone wrong. He reclined his seat and lay back, out of sight.

Rule number one: in order to be a better man, he'd had to stay away from women.

But May, breathing gravel dust and thinking of the animals in her tub, had seen him first. Or thought she had. She looked, saw a man; looked again, saw an empty car. She didn't trust her eyes. If there was a man, she thought, he was probably drunk. Passed out. Unaware of the rocking of his car, the wind, the radio that, as she got closer, she could hear was still on. If she let him be, he might stay passed out until his car wrapped itself around a tree, or flew into the bar behind him.

When May peered into the car window with a cupped hand, she was shocked to see the man staring up at her. Then his eyes were closed. May rapped on the window.

"You okay?" she said. She recognized this man. She didn't like him. He'd been thrown out of Saving Grace.

Ames didn't open his eyes. He pictured the woman's eyes, blue as a row of detached corneas he'd seen once in the life science classroom. The corneas had been floating in baby jars of formaldehyde, but Ames hadn't been able to shake the feeling that they still could see him. No matter where he stood, the corneas seemed to be watching.

May could tell he was faking. His closed eyelids kept trying to blink. He'd seen her. He hadn't been asleep.

He faked a yawn. He stretched his bare arms.

Eight o'seven: sunset.

The tornado was tearing the guts out of an old silo. No remorse for its owners, huddled in an underground shelter, listening to the metal wail. Later, the family described the sound as an explosion, but that belied the awful quiet that existed underground. The loudest sound was their own breathing. The father held the ears of his two boys. The livestock were singing.

Seven miles away, Trooper's dogs chewed metal. His daughter held a flashlight, read a woman's magazine that was too old for her. His wife's thumb moved repetitively over the back of his hand. His skin there ached, but he didn't withdraw the hand. He felt bad about Ames. On the drive home, the sky in Trooper's rearview had blackened fast, and Trooper was especially sensitive to veiled forms of cruelty. He hadn't meant to be cruel. Still, when he'd come home and explained to his wife about the delay, she'd said, "Poor guy. He probably doesn't have anywhere to go." Trooper had felt immediately sorry.

He took his wife's other hand, and her thumb on that side began working, too. The mattress, one he'd pulled straight off the bed, smelled like detergent and made him sleepy. The three of them listened to the dogs together.

Trooper would back the cops later. He'd say May must've gone west. But his face wouldn't believe it. His face would say: take the worst thing you can imagine, and that's what Ames did.

Another story says this.

Ames held one hand over May's mouth, while he tried to get off with the other. He wouldn't have killed her in the act. He killed her afterwards because he couldn't do it. Because even that, the worst of his desires, had deserted him. That's when the real anger hit. He could almost fit his whole hand around her neck. He didn't believe she was dying, even when her tongue pushed out from between her teeth. He felt better when it was over. He didn't need to struggle. His head cleared.

May felt the tornado in the ground. She felt her eyes bulge. The pressure of Ames's hand was rough, but his skin was soft. He was the kind of man who'd never farmed or worked in a factory. Even at her most desperate, a small part of her was grateful for that: the soft hands of a violent man. Her body went into panic mode—accelerated heart rate, adrenaline—but her mind refused to follow. She was still on her way to church. She just couldn't find it.

Ames dragged May's body into the abandoned fields behind the bar. There were plenty of old tools lying around, more blowing in from the Tractor Graveyard. Grave digging would've been hard work for a guy like Ames, but he was running on fear by then. The tornado was coming, and came, in fact, in the middle of the burial. When it hit, he lay flat on the ground, watched objects fly around him: trash cans, doors, rakes. The experience left him untouched. All the holes he'd had were still in place. He was still afraid. He still had to heap dirt upon a grave. He still, in the midst of it all, wanted to be a better man.

Crazy, that two girls from eastern Alabama would meet in Arizona. Hundreds of miles from the Mason-Dixon line, they'd created a life alone, without relatives. They figured it was just as well. They didn't get out of Phoenix much. They still ate grits, fried their vegetables, watched the sky. They still got quiet when the weather changed. They had a small, tan house with too-green grass and a small cotton field out back. They'd been surprised and somewhat comforted to find that cotton grew in the desert. It was, they figured, enough of a relative for them.

When the doorbell rang one night, they weren't expecting a soul. They were eating dinner. Jill got up to answer; Ana put down her fork. They'd been talking about the new irrigation system in the field, how it made the air in the house wet. Made the bread mold. Ana listened for familiar voices. Water droplets slid down windows, and the setting sun turned them red.

"Who is it?" she called to Jill. She heard laughing, a shocked sound.

"Ana, come in here," Jill said. She appeared wide-eyed in the doorway. "It's your mother."

"How on earth—" Ana said, pushing her chair back and craning around Jill to see.

"She said she flew in yesterday evening. But she doesn't have bags or anything."

"She doesn't fly," Ana said. "She never has."

"What I know," Jill said, shaking her head, "is that she's here now." And she guided Ana towards the door.

"I'm on my way to church," May said when Ames rolled down his window. It was getting late. The sun was gone. May had shifted her flashlight around so the handle of it was free—a weapon, if she needed it. She slept with her doors unlocked at night, but she wasn't stupid. She read the news. She watched Oprah.

"Okay," Ames said.

"Do you need help?"

"No," Ames said.

He'd tried to let her go. He had.

May knew she should've left right then. She could just make it to the church. But she didn't leave. He looked so pathetic, lying there in his beat-up car. He looked like he didn't know any better. May opened the car door.

"Come on," she said, taking his arm. "Let's get out of here."

"I can drive," Ames said. Her sudden touch made his mouth gummy.

"No, thanks," May said.

Ames let her hoist him out of the car, and it took a long time. She wedged one foot in the door, propped his arm on her knee, pulled him out. He went. He was sweating. He pulled hard on her wrist when she helped him up. She held onto the flashlight.

"Watch it," she said.

They cut through the asparagus field. May thought she could see the vegetables breathing. Gorging themselves. Heavy stalks lit, as if from inside. They heard a sound like a highway. Then a train.

"Oh, shit," Ames yelled, trudging through the clay, "you stupid bitch. It's coming." He wheeled around and ran for his car, leaving May alone in the field.

Perhaps Ames did have repulsive intentions. He claimed he never had a chance to try anything with May before the tornado came, and people were willing to believe that. There was no evidence. Ames said he hadn't made it back to his car. He'd collapsed in the field, and screamed. He could only assume May had done the same, but that she hadn't survived. Maybe she'd been torn to shreds, he said meanly. Maybe she'd evaporated.

A week later, Ames was arrested for stealing money from the pawn shop. People were willing to believe the impossible, but not that he was innocent.

May held fast to the plants on her left and right. She smelled dirt and clay, and something metallic, like a rusty bicycle. The tornado was in the ground. It was not part of the sky, after all. It was part of the land.

When things quieted down, May opened her eyes and found that she was not in the field. She had plants in her hands, but she was in the middle of the thing. She could see straight up to the oval of sky at the top. On the thick walls, rapid-fire lightning struck. In the vortex, mini-tornadoes whirled. They bounced off each other and the debris they'd gathered. May was airborne, and yet still. It was surprisingly bright.

May let go. She dropped the grass in her hands, and floated.

Some people say May was redeemed. Reclaimed. That she was holy.

Some say she moved to Arizona.

Ames went to jail for theft. It was a kind of relief. For days afterward, the air fizzed like soda pop. Every explanation he gave was different. He seemed as confused as anybody about what had happened. He had no sense for a story, and maybe that was his worst crime of all.

There are the puppies. There are the two phone calls. There is the way we're more willing to believe the impossible than the tragic. The way we understand more about each other than, maybe, we ever want to admit.

all the america you want

When the first bulldozers rattled into South Tampa after the Urban Renewal Act went into effect, half the residents cheered. They were the ones who'd voted for the Act, who remembered promises of clean apartments, new sidewalks, grass. They stood outside in church clothes or fast food uniforms and believed that the lord—or at least the city council— had finally provided. Behind them stood those who'd voted against the Act, or who hadn't voted at all. They kept one eye on the grinding machinery and one on their front doors. They slouched and made nervous jokes: "They're coming for your place, Rocco."

A year later, demolition had become as standard a feature of the neighborhood as chain link fences. If the city wasn't razing someone's apartment building, it was converting old duplexes into casitas, rustic-looking split-levels that gangs of teenage protesters promptly set on fire. The residents packed their couches into pickup trucks and accepted short-term leases in places that already had For Sale signs in the windows. Em, who'd lived there almost her whole life, had voted for the Act last spring. Now she was mad enough to light a few casitas on fire herself.

"It's like we're living in a war zone," she told Daniel, her sixteen-year-old half-brother who still lived with their mother. "Three families are living outside my apartment. One of them set up a bed on the sidewalk."

Daniel turned off the machine he'd been using to slice a round of ham and wiped his hands on a Meat Market apron. Em had stopped by to see him on her way home from Merry Maids, where she cleaned houses. Daniel had just come on his shift.

"There's a kid in my building who calls it a war," he said. "He's one of the casita vandals. He said they torch the inside first. They run a line of gas from the front door to the back."

"The inside *first*," Em said. "Smart." She'd been lucky—her complex opened onto the highway and faced an all-night liquor store. The liquor store had held its ground, and Em's place had been spared.

"You got to do something," Daniel said. "Fight back or whatever. Fuckers aren't going to leave anything behind." He spat into a steel sink, and the faucet washed away yellow mucus. "The playground, man," he said.

After four evictions, Daniel and their mother had landed across from it. Gandy Playground. Em had raised her brother there, eating stolen Cracker Jack on the swings, listening to Bobby Brown on her mother's boom box, watching Daniel through the passenger-seat window while she fooled around in parked cars—first with boys, then girls, too—and later, breaking up fights he picked with other boys even when those boys outweighed him. That morning, on her way to work, Em had seen dump trucks loaded with slide and tire back out of the four-car parking lot.

Tonight, the black curls on Daniel's forehead framed a tight brow, eyes that darted from Em to the floor when he talked about the casita vandals—his third mention of them in a week. Em knew kids like Daniel didn't need a reason to riot. Just growing up here was enough to make you want to burn things down.

"Let it go," Em said, as much to herself as to her brother. "It won't do any good to get worked up."

"Bullshit," Daniel said. "What won't do any good is waiting around to get fucked up the ass." He wiped his forehead and looked at Em. "Sorry," he said.

"It's okay," Em said. "I don't get fucked up the ass."

Daniel had been around Em's girlfriends—Leslie, Heather, Rita: the playground flings—since he was born. He was the least squeamish about them now. Their mother hadn't found out until high school, when the police had caught Em and Rita half-dressed behind the dumpster. Their mom had been upset—more because Rita was white than because she was a girl.

"You can act fruity," she'd told Em, "but don't be dumb. Stick to your own."

Em's birth had been the product of such stupidity. Her mother had locked eyes with a white man in Havana and nine months later carried his child over the sea alone. The second time she'd done it right. Daniel's dad was Cuban, and he'd at least had the courtesy to leave a phone number. Both children knew their fathers only by the traits they left behind: Em got the snooty attitude, her mother said; Daniel got the temper. Neither could speak Spanish well, and Em's skin was so light she could pass if she felt like it. When their mother was very angry at the two of them, she accused them of being *residents* here. It was her most severe insult.

"What I mean," Em said to her brother at the Meat Market, "is you should leave that shit alone. There are enough people in jail for no reason."

Daniel thrust a white package of the ham at Em, marked at a quarter of its original price. She could smell the salty meat through the paper. She waited for Daniel to promise that he'd stay out of the casitas.

He grinned, a flash of crooked teeth. "Me?" he said finally. "I'm just the butcher."

After the dump trucks, the construction crews slunk in. They set up Port-o-Lets on the site of the playground, and three men in business suits—architects, maybe, Em wasn't sure—stood around pointing at the empty land. When Em passed in her Merry Maids uniform, they surveyed her with approval. She crossed to the other side of the street. The laborers arrived next, carpenters and pipe fitters and cement masons, and they catcalled to Em from atop their machinery. She still crossed to the other side of the street.

The clatter vibrated through the neighborhood for weeks until one day a mortar and wood skeleton rose from the ground, first two, then three times the size of anything in the vicinity. Large and abrupt as a chain furniture store. People in the surrounding apartments set up folding chairs in their parking lots to watch the construction, and Em's mother handed out Miller Lights in cans. Once, on her way home from work—her elbows and knees aching from scrubbing tubs—Em stopped to take one.

"That building is going to be somebody's house," her mother said, nodding across the street. "Believe that?"

Em took a seat on the curb next to her brother, who was leaning back on his hands, a beer can between his knees. Em had cleaned eight houses that day, rubbed beads of Old English into eight dining room tables, scoured mildew from the grout in ten showers. The spot between her shoulder blades ached. The yellow calluses on her fingers had begun to split.

Em's mother turned back to a conversation with a man she called Red Hat. Others in the circle continued, too, speaking without addressing anyone as though they were used to being ignored. "I'll bet that's the kitchen," one said, pointing to a pile of wooden beams. The others nodded. Then later, "Nah, that's just the bathroom." They spent whole days in lawn chairs, went home to fourth-floor walkups without air conditioning. Their bathrooms were in their kitchens.

Em lived in an apartment three blocks away that had graffiti in the form of state maps spray painted on the walls. South Dakota, Washington, Missouri. She'd seen this tag other places, on overpasses and the brick sides of warehouses, but she didn't know the artist, or where that artist lived now. She liked to trace with her fingers the bold eastern border of Tennessee, the sloping mountain range across northern Arizona. Sometimes when she was drunk or high, Em sat on the floor of her bedroom closet where the walls were bare, and she doodled her name in bubble letters. One day she would draw her own map—there were a few states the previous tenant had left out.

"That's the *Florida* room," Em's mother said, pointing. "Right there. My cousin has one of those in Miami. Everybody has one of those in Miami. Some people have two."

"A Florida room," Red Hat said. He pulled a Marlins cap over his eyes. "What do I know? I just live here."

Em's mother grunted. "Not for long."

Across the street, a brown-skinned woman in a blue blazer, probably a few years older than Em, stepped out of an SUV and began making notes on one of the businessmen's clipboards. She shook her head, smacked the clipboard into the man's chest. Then she shouted to a worker on the second floor.

"She's the owner," Em's mother said. "Puerto Rican, but she's from Miami. I think she works for the city."

"You sure have a lot of information," Em said.

Her mother sighed loudly. "My eyes are open, aren't they?"

Em watched the woman circle the house twice, knock at a crossbeam with her fist, and scribble on the clipboard. The businessmen watched her, too, without seeming to stare. Em liked the way this woman directed the men around her. The way she wore a hard hat with ease.

When the woman noticed the onlookers across the street, she muttered something to the man next to her, who laughed. Then she strode towards them, heading straight for Em. Her shoes were the exact shade of her blazer. Her haircut, while not exactly stylish, looked expensive.

"I'm Mandy," she said, stopping several feet short of the curb. "That's my house those gringos are fucking up."

No one laughed. Mandy caught Em's eye and said, "You can't trust white men with nothing." Em looked down at her brother's stained tennis shoe.

"Y'all live around here?" Mandy tried again.

"No," Em's mother said. She pointed at the parking lot. "We live here."

"And you don't," Daniel said. "So fuck off."

"I don't live here," Em said.

"Shut up, Em," Em's mother said. "You do, too."

Mandy nodded. She stepped back into the line of traffic, and an approaching driver honked. She didn't move out of the way. "You have a right to be angry," she said. "I'm on your side. The casitas, man. What a dumb-ass idea."

"Your house," Em said, "is no casita." She'd meant it as a joke, but it came out sounding confrontational. "That the only one you got?"

"The only one I'm going to live in," Mandy said. "But I own three more lots in town."

"Three more," Em's mother said. "Good for you." The men in the folding chair circle chuckled.

"I know you have no reason to trust me," Mandy said. "But understand this: I'm not going to lie to you. I'm building here, and that means some things will change, but I'm not here to chase you out. I plan on spending a lot of money to make this a better place. For all of us. And I'm going to watch over your complex, here. Make sure nobody touches it. I can do that for you."

After a long pause, Em laughed quietly. "It's not that we don't appreciate it," she said. "It's just a really shitty complex."

"I can make it better," Mandy said. She looked at Daniel, seemed to make a mental note of something. "And I will," she said before heading back across the street. "I'll make it better."

When she was gone, everyone relaxed, relived the conversation on their own terms: "Talking about how she's going to *give* us the place," Red Hat said. "Thanks, but I'll take hers."

Daniel said he didn't care who she worked for, her house was worse than the casitas. Trash, he called it. Ugly money. "From people," he said, "who should know better."

Em pulled the beer away from Daniel and took a swig. She understood resentment, but she didn't know what Daniel thought he was protecting. As though he wouldn't trade the whole place for just one of Mandy's vaulted rooms.

"Speaking of people," Em said, "I heard some kids lit another casita on fire. Brilliant job, I heard. The house is totaled."

"How about that," Daniel said.

Em laughed again. She couldn't tell, sometimes, whether her brother was a very young boy or a politician. She kept the beer, stretched, and groaned. She wanted to follow Mandy across the street and tell her that saving the complex was a nice thing to do.

A dumb thing, maybe, preserving the habitat of people who hated you, but a nice thing. But to follow Mandy would've been to make her mother and brother look like the helpless fucks they were, so instead she went home and downed the last six-pack in her fridge, practiced writing her name in the corner of her closet. She slept curled against the door, dreaming about work: grimy carpets and soiled sheets, mantels covered in thin layers of dust that would not stick to her rag, that blew into the air, swirled around, and settled.

The house grew, sometimes in increments, sometimes overnight. Wood, then drywall, then yellow brick. Yellow. A sun of a house, Em said, and by the time the sod was being laid around the circular driveway, that was what everyone was calling it: the Sun House. It was poles apart from the identical blue-sided houses with screened-in pools that Em cleaned in the suburbs. The Sun House had a Spanish façade that resembled the style of the old duplexes, or what their style must've been before they'd succumbed to the grit and rot of neglect. Bay windows arched under curling wrought iron. Two columns supported the towering second story, composed, rumor had it, of stone flown in from Barcelona. Em pictured the house while she mopped footprints off the Reynoldses' tile kitchen, or as she ran a dry cloth over the Gonzalezes' wedding pictures. She imagined lights in the upstairs windows. She imagined chandeliers.

Nights, Em visited one of two gay bars on Kennedy Boulevard where the women were sad and jovial, often at the same time, and were always outnumbered by the men. One of them was usually willing to go home with Em—if not a patron, then Iris, the blonde bartender at Fusion who served Em free double shots if she were alone. Em blew her paychecks on speeding tickets and strip clubs, once going through three hundred dollars watching a belly dancer who was cool with girls. She stayed all night, drank herself blind, and went home poorer, she thought, than anyone should rightly be.

Then Em got her notice. She'd been waiting for it so long that it'd almost ceased to be a real threat, but there it was, a carbon copy stuck in her door. Eviction. The notice gave Em three months—more time than usual, which Em attributed to problems with the liquor store—and provided the names of several complexes in the area that had vacancies. Her mother's place, with its tiny, windowless apartments and dank-smelling walls, was not listed.

Em spent the night at Fusion drinking tequila and avoiding the subject of her apartment. When the bar closed at two, she and Iris stumbled to Taco Bell and spent their last sixty cents on a burrito. On their way out, Iris said, "If you could pick anywhere to go right now, where would it be?" Em didn't even need to think.

The Sun House was completed but not occupied—the workers had packed up and left that afternoon. The thick lawn was so cool it felt damp. Gnats zigzagged across the security lights. Iris had hot sauce in her hair when she leaned into the grass and said, "Why here?"

Em put her head in Iris's lap and gazed up at the whirling night. "Because it feels like being someplace else," she said.

"We could go somewhere," Iris said. "Run away together. In four hours we could be in Miami."

It was an old joke: everyone in South Tampa was on the way out. Once they stopped smoking/drinking/snorting. Once they saved enough money. Once they passed the GED. Once their wife/kids/father came over.

Iris stroked Em's hairline. The house floated above them, immense and naked. The security lights lining the driveway seemed an inadequate armor.

"We could be there by morning," Iris murmured.

Em had never been on a vacation. She'd never gotten in her car and driven four hours just to be someplace else. She'd lived in Orlando one summer, but that was for a job, when she'd swept gum wrappers at Lake Buena Vista and lived in her car and gotten methodically ignored by hundreds of tourists a day. After three months she'd figured that in Tampa, at least she had family.

"And then we'd be there," Em said.

"With no money and no place to go," Iris said. "I know."

"And it'd be South Tampa all over again."

"South Tampa's not so bad."

"It wouldn't be," Em said, "if you could ever leave it."

Iris had made enough money tending bar to move out of the neighborhood and into a studio apartment a block away from the bay. Her place had working appliances, a wooden balcony, and clean, white walls. Em had only seen it twice. Usually Iris insisted they go to Em's place—she said she felt more comfortable. At her place, she was constantly referring to the security deposit. Em could hardly sit on the toilet seat for fear she'd ruin Iris's chance at the security deposit.

"Let's peek in the windows," Em said. "Let's try the doors. Let's write graffiti on the walls."

Iris pulled Em on top of her. The air was wet, and Iris's hair smelled like fast food. When Em reached under Iris's shirt, there were damp hollows beneath her breasts. They fooled around quickly and with purpose until one of Em's legs flopped onto the brick walkway and a number of bright lights clicked on. "Shit," Iris said, scrambling for her shirt. "Land mines."

"It's just lights," Em said. But she felt caught. She wiped her hands on her jeans and buttoned up. Her back itched from the grass, and she felt mosquito bites swelling on her neck. Across the street, she could see shadows of boys standing in the upstairs hallway of her mother's apartment building. If Iris asked now, Em would say she wanted to go someplace exotic—Aruba or the Bahamas. Someplace so far away it seemed not really to exist at all.

"One of these days we'll do it," Em said. "We'll drive away."

"We will," Iris said. She took Em's hand.

They held hands all the way down the lawn. As soon as they stepped into the darkness beyond the lighted driveway, they let go, instinctively crossing their arms in front of their chests.

The three moving trucks that edged onto the street in front of the Sun House the next day took up an entire block. Five men spent all day unloading them, lugging mahogany tables and couches and cardboard boxes through the front door. When Em left for work in the morning, they were hauling bedroom furniture; by the time she got off at eight, they were finishing the kitchen. Homeless families who'd set up camp outside her mother's building watched wearily behind the folding chair brigade. Em's mother waved her over.

"What do you know about that Mandy girl?" she said without even offering Em a beer. She pointed to where Mandy was standing with her hands on her hips just outside the garage.

"She's young, but she ain't pretty," one of the men said.

"She's rich," Red Hat said. "She don't need to be pretty."

Em looked across the street. They were right: she wasn't pretty. Her features were too long for her face, her nose was angular, and half her chin disappeared into her neck. Her brown skin was the color of her thin hair. She looked strong in the legs, though, which Em admired.

"What I heard," Em said, "is what you've told me."

Her mother rolled her eyes, put a beer can to her forehead and cursed in Spanish. "Grow up," she said. "Listen to me: she's your kind of girl."

"What kind of girl is that?" Em said.

"I hear—" her mother nodded to Red Hat—"she doesn't like men."

Across the street, Mandy tipped the movers. They shoved the money in their pants without counting it. "I'll bet," Em said.

"Shut up," her mother said. "I'm telling you." She pulled Em's face so they were eye to eye. "No more screwing around with white women," she said, and Em wondered how much of the date with Iris her mother had witnessed from across the street. "Get you something better." She swatted Em's rear.

"Sure," Em said. "I'll invite myself over."

"Wait here," her mother said. "She'll come. She always does."

Em's mother was right. Once the movers had eased their trucks back into the street, Mandy headed across. "She does this every day?" Em said, but the group had gone silent.

"Good to see you, Emilia," Mandy said when she arrived. Em glanced at her mother, who wordlessly handed Mandy a beer.

"Em," Em said.

"Your mom says you clean houses. How long have you been doing that?"

"Too long," Em said without smiling. She half expected Mandy to follow up with, *So, you're a dyke, right?*

"And how's your living situation?" Mandy said.

Em dropped her eyes. It was the one question people in the neighborhood didn't ask. They might talk generally about casitas or the growing crowd of homeless people living outside their windows, but they avoided subjects that might make someone lower her eyes. Em had told no one, not even Iris, about the eviction. But she was sure everyone in the circle had seen the liquor store, empty now, and knew what that meant for Em.

"Fine," Em said. "I'm one of the lucky ones."

"Good." Mandy stood up tall. "I've been talking to your mom and her friends about supporting local businesses. You're my neighbors, my people. I want to invest in you. I don't want to pay some white girl to clean my house. I'd rather pay you, Em."

She was addressing everyone—the folding chair group, the street, the entire complex. She might as well have had a podium. She smiled so big that, in spite of how she'd offended her, Em felt like clapping. "When do you think that check will be coming?" she said, raising an eyebrow.

Mandy raised one back. "Maybe when my house gets dirty."

"I don't know," Em said. "All that building dust, those workers' hands on everything. I'd say you're due."

Mandy looked around the group, then pointed a finger at Em. "You're on," she said. "Next week. I'll call." She waited for a break in traffic and darted across the street.

Em's mother laughed out loud. "That's what I'm talking about," she said. "That's my girl."

Her first day at the Sun House, a Tuesday, Em woke up an hour early. She dressed in the brown company polo a size too small that showed off her chest, put on lipstick, and rubbed vegetable oil on her eyelids. She walked by the Meat Market, and though she saw Daniel through the deli window, she didn't stop. He hated the Sun House worse each time she spoke to him. Since he lived across from it, he had to view its strange daylight glow whenever he stepped outside. The last time she'd visited him, he'd been bug-eyed and shaky.

"Damn yellow house," he'd said. "Always shining in my window."

"The security lights?" Em said.

"Yeah. I'd like to take a hammer to those lights."

So, although she was sure he must've heard by then from her mother, Em didn't tell Daniel about her good fortune. She didn't tell him how she strolled to the house that first day, or how she walked right up to the front door like she meant business. How, when Mandy let her in, Em stood in the foyer disappointed that there was track lighting instead of chandeliers. Mandy looked almost sweet in cut-offs and a Miami Dolphins T-shirt. Em immediately pictured her in bed, and the image was not unsatisfying.

The Sun House had rooms decorated in ways no one in the folding-chair circle could've predicted. They were enormous and smelled like fresh paint. As she followed Mandy upstairs, Em felt giddy at her good luck. Mandy showed her the library lined with bookcases, pointing out a wall dedicated solely to Latin American History; she led Em through the bedroom, sleigh bed piled high with pillows, air purifier humming quietly in the corner; and they passed through the study, where a thickly polished desk supported a nine-part computer system. They stopped in a rec room filled with plastic blow-up furniture and paper lamps, a stoplight on the wall that changed every minute, a sixty-gallon aquarium full of frilly fish.

"They're fake," Mandy said, pulling one out. It made swimming motions in the air. "They have motion sensors so they don't wreck into each other." The fish was iridescent with pinstripes of gold across its middle. When Mandy replaced it, it continued making calculated circles around the tank, swerving lightly to avoid the others. "The guy who sells them is nuts," Mandy said. "He's got a contract with Sea World to make a whole ocean of these, life-sized. The predators really eat the prey."

"And then what?" Em said.

"Then somebody separates them, and they start all over."

"I'd like to see that," Em said.

When they finished the tour, Mandy invited Em to stay for lemonade, which they drank at the kitchen nook in front of glass doors to the garden. Mandy sat close enough that their knees almost touched. Em could see a few wiry strands of gray in her hair, though her skin was as smooth as the tile floor. Outside, azaleas were blooming in such profusion they were almost too much to look at.

"I like your flowers," Em said.

"Azaleas," Mandy said. "Such drama queens."

"They're nice," Em said. She wished she knew prettier words, longer ones with more syllables. When she spoke, she felt very aware of her mouth.

Mandy stood, slid open the glass door and called to Em from the porch. Along the side of the house, a dozen more potted plants were in full bloom. "Take one," Mandy said.

Em chose a hibiscus, red flowers dripping bright yellow stamens. She held the plant close to her face and breathed deeply. It smelled like nothing, but Em's head swam.

"It's beautiful," she said. "The whole place is beautiful." She meant it. Usually clients showed Em the broom closet, told her to mop under the table and not touch anything on the mantel and remember the toilets. Some women spoke in rapid Spanish that Em had trouble following.

"Where are you from?" one, irritated, would ask.

"Here," Em would say.

"Where's your mother from?"

"Cuba," Em would say, and the owner would nod, go silent, and speak to Em in English from then on.

But Mandy was different. And on Em's way out, Mandy touched her arm. "What do you do for fun around here?" she said.

Em looked out the door at the brilliant, damp lawn. "We go somewhere else."

"I'm going stir crazy," Mandy said.

"There's nothing to do here but work and sleep," Em said. "And eat."

"Then we'll do that," Mandy said. "We'll eat."

Em made the first move. She thought. Later it seemed like they'd both been working their own angles, missing each other through three dinners, then striking, physically, the first time they slept together. Em spent her days becoming familiar with the Sun House, finding light switches and outlets, silverware drawers and linen closets, until she'd memorized them by touch. Then Mandy would invite her over for dinner in the evenings, and Em would stay long into the night. Once, after a meal of swordfish steaks, they retired to the room with fake fish to watch TV and Em put her arm around Mandy's neck. She toyed with Mandy's bra strap while Mandy told her about two properties she'd sold, and the contracts she'd gotten for four more lots. "The one thing you can rely on," she said, "is the value of cheap land."

Em had been planning her move all day, though afterwards her timing seemed awkward. She felt mad and desperate—cheap land, indeed—so that, when they finally kissed, she was more aggressive than usual. She pushed her face into Mandy's and took a handful of the sofa behind her head. Then Mandy's hands found their way underneath Em's shirt, and Em relaxed into the rhythm of the room, the small noises of the couch, the breath of the air conditioning. Mandy knew what she was doing. She and Em moved well together, and fast, all tongues and fingers. Em forgot about her job, her apartment, her brother. For a long time, Em was aware only of the soft spaces on her knees, belly, and palms—the places where she and Mandy touched. Afterwards, Mandy seemed smaller, more like the other women Em knew. They fell asleep with the TV still on.

At midnight, Em woke to the sound of breaking glass. The crashes echoed and bounced through the rooms from somewhere outside. Em opened her eyes, startled by how far away the ceiling looked. "Mandy," she said. "Wake up." She turned, but Mandy's eyes were already open.

"They've been at it a while," Mandy said. "I don't think they're breaking in." She'd been lying flat under a blanket, her head a dark spot on the cushion, but now she got up and slid into a pair of shorts that were lying on the floor. "I'm going to look."

"Don't," Em said. She turned toward the window and listened for familiar voices. The crashes were interspersed with yells now, hoots of excitement that blended together. Four, maybe five of them. They weren't trying to be quiet.

Mandy returned, and they both lay down, Mandy with the shorts still on. She looked calm. "It's the security lights," she said. "They're smashing them."

"Are you going to call the cops?" Em said.

Mandy sighed, her shoulders slumped. "They're only kids," she said. "They don't know any better."

"No," Em said. "They know better. They know better than to smash somebody's security lights with a hammer."

"A hammer?" Mandy said.

Em shrugged.

Mandy played with one of Em's toes, bent down and kissed it. "You'd tell me if you knew anything about this," she said. "Even if you only heard something. Right?"

"Yes," Em said, too fast. Tomorrow morning, she decided. She'd visit the Meat Market. She'd buy new security lights. She'd make herself clear.

"Kids in these neighborhoods," Mandy said. "They can't see the big picture. They defend run-down houses and half-ass jobs like there's nothing else. I don't know how to explain it to them."

Em imagined Sun Houses sprouting up in all the dingiest parts of her neighborhood: the liquor store, the boarded-up community center. Her own apartment complex. But when she tried to think of the big picture, she had a hard time imagining anyone she knew in it.

"They don't understand," Mandy said. "They think I'm running them out."

"Maybe you're not running them out," Em said. "But somebody is."

"You could talk to them," Mandy said. "You could find out who they are. Not to punish them. Just to talk. Maybe they'd listen to you."

"They listen," Em said.

"I need you." Mandy put her hand on Em's chest, and Em felt her heart give way. "If I ignore this, I'm afraid it'll get worse. That they'll break in. Hurt me. Us."

"No," Em whispered. "They wouldn't do that."

"I could pay you," Mandy said, and the room closed in around Em. "Like a translator." She fell silent, and the only sound in the room was the humming of the aquarium, like ears listening, or machines breathing. "They're gone," Mandy said.

Em put her arm around Mandy's shoulders, and Mandy buried her face in Em's shirt. "I don't want to get hurt," Mandy said.

"I don't want them to hurt you," Em said. She held onto Mandy's shoulders. "I'll see what I can find out."

Mandy was quiet for a long time, and when she started to breathe heavily, Em thought maybe she was crying. But Mandy's eyes were closed and her mouth had fallen open. Em slid out from beneath her. She plunged a hand into the tank and removed a gold fish. She could feel the motor buzzing in her hand. She was halfway home when it finally stilled.

At the Meat Market, nothing had changed. Daniel was slicing turkey. He didn't look up when Em came in.

"I know what you've been doing," she said.

"I haven't done anything," Daniel said. Em watched the turkey fall from one side of the slicer. She tried to relax her jaw. He was in high school. Like Mandy had said, he was only a kid.

"You're right about that," Em said. "Don't kid yourself. You haven't changed anything."

There were long pauses between everything the two of them said, and in between only the noise of the supermarket:

cash drawers dinging open. Bland pop music barely loud enough to hear. Clerks, young and old, wearing ruts into the floor. Em wanted more than this for her brother. She wanted more for herself.

"All I have to say," Daniel said, "is watch your back."

"I clean her house," Em said. "It's my job."

Daniel turned to her, and the look on his face made Em step back, as if from something too hot. "I bet she pays you good," he said.

Em shivered. Daniel sliced turkey as easily as he destroyed houses. Em wanted to hit him, to pull him across the counter and shake him. "I *like* her," she said. "What do you want me to do?"

"She's trash," Daniel said. "I want you to leave her. Help me."

Em backed away from the counter. "No," she said. "I can't."

"Then watch your back," Daniel said.

Em brought the matter to their mother. From inside the Sun House, Em had spotted her sometimes, leaving in a Pancake House uniform or sitting outside with Red Hat. Em had tried to be discreet about her night-time visits to the Sun House, but privacy didn't matter anymore. She'd been kidding herself that privacy had ever existed.

She waited until she saw her mother exit the city bus. Em stood on the porch of the Sun House, feeling its glory behind her, and waved.

Her mother, shoulders low, waved back. "Not like it's yours," she said.

Inside the apartment, she offered Em coffee with milk and told her to stay out of other people's business.

"He's going to get in trouble," Em said. "He's going to drag us all down with him."

Em's mother touched her leg. "Is it nice over there? Is she good to you?"

"It's nice," Em said. "She's nice."

Her mother blew into her coffee, touched her palm to her temple. Her shirt was thin, and the collar hung low on her chest. She was sweating a little, in the nape of her neck. The mug she'd handed Em said Crawford's Wrecking Crew. Em wondered where she'd gotten it.

"Your brother is angry," her mother said. "We're all angry." She waved her words away. "It'll pass. It doesn't really matter."

"It isn't going to pass," Em said. "Not until he does something awful. He'll go to jail."

"He's fighting back." Her mother chuckled and looked away from Em. "He thinks he has the right."

"He'll go to jail," Em repeated, each word like a proclamation.

"He makes his decisions," her mother said. "You make yours." She set down her coffee cup, and Em knew it was time to go.

Daniel made the evening news, but only as part of a gang of teenagers that police credited with the weekend sabotage of over a dozen casitas. "Smoke covers the streets of South Tampa," the reporter said against a backdrop of fire trucks, "in a good plan gone terribly wrong."

Em watched her back. One night, walking home late from the Sun House, she saw her brother riding a bike slowly with two other boys, all dirty jeans and low voices. They fell silent when they saw her, and Em crossed to the other side of the street. They smelled like something raw, between flesh and food. They didn't speak to her, but they looked, and the looks were full of foul language.

"They tore down the Sea Breeze," Em told Mandy at dinner one Thursday, two weeks before her eviction. She hadn't found a new place yet; all the places listed on the notice were full. More homeless people had lined the outsides of buildings, and the police came by several times a day to break up fights. The Sea Breeze had been one of the vacant places, a dilapidated apartment complex across from Em's building. People had lived there for a night or a week as they passed through. In high school, Em had lived there herself after fights with her mother. The complex stank of piss and heat, and there were dark stains on the ground, walls, and beds. Messages scrawled in pen on the ceiling. For six days, she'd written notes on the walls. For six nights, someone had answered her. *I want to meet you*, she'd scribbled, and the stranger had written back, *You can't have everything you want.* Em had wandered in and out of empty rooms, finding the same thing on the inside of each unlocked door: used sheets. Needles. Fast food bags and cockroaches. Trash. Over the years, she'd glimpsed other people emerging from the building, strung out and empty-eyed, barely human. Moving on.

Now it was gone, crushed. Nobody would mourn the Sea Breeze except the homeless. Em wondered if the construction crews had bothered to evacuate.

"They?" Mandy said. "Oh, hon. That's one of mine."

"It's right across from my place," Em said. Then she caught herself, too late.

"Shit," Mandy said. "Em."

"One of yours?"

"I didn't know."

Mandy had never been to Em's apartment. After that first day, she'd never asked about it. She'd given Em the hibiscus bush, a floor lamp, a framed photograph of the mountains—but she didn't know that the hibiscus had died, or that the lamp looked ridiculous, or that to hang the photo Em would've had to cover up most of the map of Tennessee, and Em had decided in favor of Tennessee. Mandy didn't know how many bedrooms Em had, or if she had air conditioning, or how good her water pressure was. Not if Em had windows or could hear the highway at night. Sometimes Em believed that she could let herself sink into Mandy's life, into her house and bed and wallet. Sometimes

Daniel's name was on her lips like a confession. But just before she said it, she'd feel the pull of the neighborhood. She'd hear the rustle of the homeless people across the street and know that she could not give him up.

"Come over," she said. "Then you'll know."

Mandy looked scared. She seemed not to have control of her hands, which floated in front of her. Her mouth twitched. She owned the world, Em thought, but she was lost in it.

"No," Mandy said. She reached for Em. "You stay here. Live with me."

"I can't make you safe," Em said. "I don't know anything."

"I don't care," Mandy said. "I want you here."

Em didn't need to return home, not really. Mandy had everything she needed. But she did go home, one last time, to draw her map. She bought two sets of permanent markers at the Meat Market, and when she was done, she went to the deli. Daniel wasn't there. The boy operating the slicer glared at Em until she left.

At her apartment, Em cleared all the Merry Maids polos out of her closet and laid the markers on the floor. Her map would not be a state. She wanted to draw the path to the Sun House.

She started at the far right corner with the Sea Breeze, two ghostlike people standing in front. She drew the Meat Market where her brother was slicing lunchmeat, the run-down complexes and housing units along the street, the oaks swinging with Spanish moss. She drew Kennedy Boulevard, its strip clubs and gay bars, the traffic and abandoned cars. She drew Iris standing at the bottom, looking fierce in black boots. She drew the sidewalks, both sides of the street, and the construction workers hooting from the windows of dump trucks. She drew Red Hat and her mother sitting in folding chairs, staring out solemnly. She drew the Sun House, large and yellow, as out of place as a yacht in a pond. And all around it, she placed remnants of Gandy Playground. Swings on the roof, a jungle gym out front, Mandy at the top of the slide in her driveway. She drew a series of dots like a string of islands and wrote MIAMI in red in the corner.

It covered the entire wall of her closet and spilled onto the sides and door. Em signed her name on the ceiling. Long, cursive letters, like ropy clouds blown in from the sea. When they demolished the building, everything Em knew about the neighborhood would go with it.

After finishing, Em packed a duffle bag and sat on the floor. She felt like she needed to say something, but she didn't know what to say, or whom to say it to. Finally, she called Iris.

"You start screwing a rich chick and forget your friends?" Iris said after Em said hello.

Em laughed. "Not forget," she said. "Just forget to call."

"I'm lonely." Iris sounded a little drunk. "Make it up to me."

When Em hesitated, Iris said, "For Christ's sake, Em, at least talk to me in person."

"Okay," Em said. "Let's go out. Like we used to. Let's celebrate."

Em hadn't been to the strip club in months, and half the employees, including the belly dancer, had quit. Women didn't stay there long. They made fast money, moved on to real jobs or fancier clubs near the bay. Em walked in with five hundred dollars cash, the accumulation of all the money Mandy had given her for spying. She'd paid Em, regardless of the kind of information she got. She'd paid Em even if Em had nothing to say.

Now Em wanted to get rid of the money. She and Iris sat at a back table and drank expensive beer—anything imported, Em told the waitress. She wanted to get drunk and confess.

"My brother is an arsonist," she told Iris.

"I know that," Iris said. "Everybody does."

"Not everybody," Em said.

Iris swayed in her seat. She fingered Em's sleeve. "Yes, she does," Iris said. "She's blind if she doesn't." Em pulled her shirt away from Iris and tilted her chair back. "Anyway," Iris said, "I came to say goodbye. I'm leaving. For real this time."

"Sure," Em said. "So am I."

"I'm serious," Iris said. "I'm already packed."

"Me, too," Em said and laughed. "I'll go with you. The Pacific, wherever."

"I never said I'd take you with me."

"No, we'll go south. As south as we can get. To the last key. Key West."

Iris began gathering up her things. "The last key is Garden Key," she said. "You have to take a boat."

"Cuba, then," Em said. She grabbed Iris's wrist. "Get in touch with my roots."

"Honey, your roots are here," Iris said. She wrenched free of Em and stood up. "There will never be anywhere else. I don't care how many Puerto Ricans you fuck, your skin is still whiter than mine."

"Get out of here," Em said.

"Say 'Hi' to your brother," Iris said. "Tell him to torch one for me."

Em sat alone in the club after Iris had gone. She stayed at the corner table ordering beer after beer in the smoky darkness, watching woman after woman pucker her lips to the spotlight and close her eyes.

Eventually one of the strippers approached her, a woman in her thirties, dressed like a genie. She told Em in Spanish that she liked to see women at the bar. That it was like working for a friend.

"No," Em said in English. "I'm from here."

"So?" the woman said in Spanish. "I'm from here, you're from here. Sit here long enough and we can be wherever you want."

She shook her shoulders. "Baby, I'll give you all the America you want."

A veil covered her nose and mouth, and another one hung over her stomach. She had green eyes and frosty red hair. Dark skin. Dark as alleys, midnight walks home, the insides of closets. "Call me Angel," she said. She breathed into Em's face through the veil, and Em saw the bouncer look once and turn away.

"Okay," Em said in halting Spanish. "I give up." She let the woman circle her mouth with her tongue, one leg inching between Em's knees. Em kept her hands at her sides—she wasn't supposed to touch. "I know you," the woman said. "My brother is friends with yours. You're Emilia Esposito."

"Call me Em," Em said. Then she rolled her eyes so far back that light shot behind her eyelids.

In the night, while Em was watching Angel make figure eights with her thighs, four boys disarmed the security system at the Sun House and broke through the sliding glass doors. Em found out later. Mandy had been in her sleigh bed, riding a fitful night's sleep, when the boys woke her and held her at knifepoint for three hours. They forced her to sit naked in the kitchen while they wrote obscenities on her skin with marker. They tore her house apart. Smashed windows, plates, mirrors. Tore books to shreds. Spray painted the inside walls: *dyke* and *rich bitch* and *motherfucker*. On the front door: *Get Out*. They pulled up carpet and tried to light the concrete underneath on fire. They burned the furniture. They scattered glass and refuse on the floor, making it slow and painful for Mandy to reach her phone once they left. They ripped her clothes. They left her with bruises on her arms, cheeks.

Em arrived just after the police. She'd heard sirens outside the strip club, and she'd hurried. Mandy was pale but not crying. She was perched on the edge of a blackened couch. She had black smudges on her arms, but Em couldn't make out any words.

"Where have you been?" Mandy said, hugging her arms to her chest. "Where the fuck have you been?"

"I was at a club," Em said. "Shit, Mandy, I was with a friend."

The room smelled like smoke and something else—sweat, adrenaline, the stink of teenage boys. An officer touched Mandy on the shoulder, and she pointed at Em. "Ask her," she said.

The officer led Em outside. He was thick-necked and sympathetic, calling Mandy Em's "friend," but looking her in the eye when he said it. They stood on the porch in front of the plowed-up yard. All around them, yellow brick was splattered with black paint.

Now that the police had arrived, people began coming out of their houses. They sat in the folding chairs in their parking lots, their eyes glassy under the street lights. They'd been inside, Em knew, watching from windows the whole time. Crouched beside the buildings. She stared back until the onlookers, glancing away, faced the beer cans in their hands. Em's mother was the only one who stared back. A warning. In her look, everything she and Em stood to lose.

She'd been out all night, she told the police. She had an alibi.

Em stayed on the porch a long time, silent. She watched people walk past, she watched until even her mother folded up her chair and went back inside. Mandy joined her after a while, stood close to Em without touching.

"The police are sending guards to the other houses," Mandy said. "They're bringing more officers to the area." She rubbed a bruise on her shoulder. "I thought you might want to know."

Em stared across the lawn, at the property line where the grass ended abruptly, replaced by thistle and sand, brown weeds too tall to support themselves. All around it, South Tampa rippled outward into a landscape that never ended. It crossed borders, oceans. Penetrated skin. Em would leave it, finally, because she had to. But it wouldn't matter. Her bones were already sun-bleached. If pierced, her veins would spill sand.

That Em hadn't known the specifics of the attack didn't matter, either. She knew what everyone else knew about the lines that'd been drawn, and which side she fell on.

"No one told me anything about this," she said.

"Fuck you," Mandy said.

Mandy left in a cloud of humidity, and Em waited on the Sun House lawn until she saw her brother walking up the street. Coming home. He was clean—no evidence except for a dark streak on his arm that could've been anything. He didn't look at the house. He didn't see Em until he'd almost passed.

"I heard they couldn't get the floor to light," Em said. She heard her brother's calmness edging into her voice and wondered if it'd always been there.

"What do you know," he said.

He turned away, but Em caught his collar. She pushed him down, throwing him off balance, and she mashed his face into the sand. She wanted him to be afraid, of himself, of her. She wanted him to know that he had no potential, that he'd move and move again and always find himself in the same place, digging in because he didn't have the brains to get out. He'd wake up to discover that the thing he'd defended so fiercely didn't love him back. A crowd gathered around her, the homeless people who lived outside her mother's building, members of the folding-chair circle, Em's mother herself. Em held her brother to the ground with her knee in his spine until the crowd, rancid and smelling of heat, finally pulled her away.

the business of souls

⤸

When I tell the story, I'm nine again on Washington Avenue. Ten, twenty, thirty years later—doesn't matter. I'm under the trailer, crushing cricket heads. A jar of live ones in my hand and a pile of bodies at my feet. It's Saturday, and a cold snap has just hit Florida. From my seat under the kitchen, I can see Dad dragging the ladder across the yard, strung along by his frozen breath.

Dad doesn't know I'm under the house. In a minute, he'll step inside where my older sister Mindy is flipping through a science catalog she swiped from junior high, and he'll expect me to be holed up with her, like we're a couple of hibernating animals. He'll march us up to the roof, one-two, and make us jump off— what he calls Landing Practice. We've done this every weekend since I could walk, and to say that Dad's an ex-paratrooper who loved jumping as much as other men loved their wives makes it a little easier to explain, but not much.

Mindy and I prefer intellectual stuff. Science. Biology, atoms and cells, plant reproduction, dissection. Every animal in our yard has gone under Mindy's steak knife, and she's even filched frogs already-preserved from the life science class. Dad threw a fit when he found frog number three in our underwear drawer, escorted us to the dumpster at the end of our street and made us pitch it in, told us never, *never* to keep dead animals in our room again. He can't see that what we're doing takes skill: peeling back the skin, snipping through the dried-up body fluids to get to the swollen organs—the heart, the stomach—careful not to pierce the gut. He doesn't know about my jar of crickets, or the ghosts of the ones I've killed that return after dark. I can hear them outside my window, flopping and scratching around, like maybe they can smell their brains on my fingertips. But I'm never brave enough to go outside and find them.

I watch Dad a few minutes, then seal the lid on my jar and duck inside, through the kitchen that doubles as his bedroom and into the room Mindy and I share.

"Dad's got the ladder," I say. Mindy's been fighting with him all day about the red lipstick she's wearing, and the Designer Imposters perfume she bought at the dollar store that Dad says makes her smell like a headache waiting to happen. I figure she could use the heads up, but she doesn't need me. She's ready. Our bottom dresser drawer is on the top bunk, full of equipment. We ought to have real gear—helmets, wrist guards, pads—but since Dad says the best protection is practice, we make do with household stuff. Knee socks and baseball caps. Publix Plastic Bandages.

"What's with you?" I ask Mindy, because normally we only suit up if it's raining, which it's not, or if I have injuries from a fight at school, which I don't, or if we're preparing for a new trick.

I haven't suggested any stunts since the last time Mindy cart-wheeled off the roof and got in white-hot trouble. Dad thinks landing is serious business, something every kid should learn, like riding a bike. He yells at us for messing around, says it's not a goddamn game. But it is a game, and Mindy and I are winning. We practice stunts off the bunk beds before we try them on the roof. I'm good at inventing new tricks; Mindy is better at executing them.

Mindy smirks. "Guess."

Lately Mindy holds enough secrets to fill a family tree, and she's just as good at keeping them. She grabs my face and squeezes my cheeks like she does when she wants to make me feel a lot younger than her. Her hands smell like a mix of Designer Imposters and formaldehyde.

"No, don't guess," she says. "Wait and see."

She unwraps the bandages we keep stocked courtesy of the Li'l Champs around the corner, where the crippled lady behind the counter won't notice Mindy in the back if I chat her up while buying Dad's weekly lotto tickets. The lady knows Dad from high school and is always saying it's a shame about our mother, who died before I could remember her. Dad says he can't stand hearing one more thing about God and Jesus and Divine Providence, so he sends us. I get this real pathetic look on my face, and the lady crumples. Mindy makes out with half the store.

When she's peeled enough bandages, Mindy says, "Ready?" and holds out her cold hands. I stick four on the lower part of each palm, where her hand would hit if she pitched forward, and one on each fingertip. She does the same to me, for luck. We pull five pairs of socks past our knees and secure the baseball hats. Hands, knees, head.

Mindy picks at a hole in the top sock when she's done. "I'm getting too old for this," she says. "One day, I'm going to tell Dad to piss off. I'll just leave. I won't come back until I'm eighteen, and maybe not even then." But when Dad pokes his head in the door, she grins like she's been missing him all day.

"Oh, Jesus," he says, looking at the socks. "What's this?"

"We're cold," Mindy says, and that shuts Dad up.

Sometimes when we're dressed in our gear, Dad shakes his head; other times he asks what will we do in a real emergency, when there's no time to tie pillows to our asses. Then there are times when he strips off the bandages in one hunk like patches of sloughed skin and throws them in the trash. Today all he says is, "Ready, Mindy? Matt?" We march outside. One-two. Dad says we look like a couple of goons with that crap on our hands, but he doesn't make us take it off. The air is wet so the bandages aren't sticking anyway.

Dad says we're learning to survive. The one thing a body ought to know is how to land on its own feet. There are days when I understand exactly what he means. I have this no-fail strategy that compensates for the fact that I've got the body of a third grader in a fifth grade class: if a kid gives me hell, I jump on him. Even if he's twice my size, landing on somebody from the top of the jungle gym or the equipment shed is bound to flatten him, and there's always some snot-nosed jerk like Tom Thornton ragging on me about living in a trailer, or having a dad for a mom, or being white because, mostly, Tom and his friends are not. Dad says their daddies don't have any more work than he does, but you wouldn't know it for the way their kids brag until you can't see straight. That's when I jam a mean fist in their mouths, because white or black or Cuban or Indian or a mix of every crappy country in the whole stinking world, I don't care, I just want to shut them up.

Dad hates the idea of fighting, mostly because of the trouble it gets me in. "Run away," he says. "That's the smart thing to do."

But around here, there's only so far you can run before Tom Thornton is at your heels, calling you worse names than you thought there were words for. And smart or not, in fifth grade there's nowhere to run that doesn't lead back to your assigned seat, your place in the alphabetical line.

Mindy says it isn't easier in junior high. Her advice is practical: hit first.

From the top of the house, I can see a long way into the distance. The air is wet, but the clouds look more like ice than rain, long and thin and white—bed sheets freezing on a clothesline. Dad says as soon as he gets a contract he'll get us winter clothes, but there's no work from here to Timbuktu for independent carpenters like him, so Mindy and I take turns with a single pair of sweat pants, and Dad thinks aloud about taking a job at the full-service car wash that advertises a hundred-dollar sign-on bonus.

I see Mindy shiver and almost feel the chill snaking up my own back. Dad doesn't notice, or pretends not to. We stand together silently, on the roof, in the cold, under the earth's clean laundry.

"Mindy," Dad says, and his voice is the one he uses to tell us about parachutes that don't open, "you go first." Usually Dad jumps first to show us how it's done, but I guess he's trying to make up with her about the perfume. "No funny business," he adds. Without looking in our direction, he raises his finger, the signal to begin. Mindy jumps. Her landing is controlled and steady, so solid her hair hardly moves. Dad yells, "Nice one," and he's proud, you can tell. Mindy says, "Thanks, Daddy," but she's looking at me.

When it's my turn I nail it, feet together, knees bent, arms at my sides like a soldier. Crickets hop away from me in the grass, and they're big and thick and just right for splitting. Mindy and I used to do that, cleave them up the middle to see what made them alive, but that was before Mindy moved on to frogs and I stopped bothering with the insides. I was never any good at dissection. I just crushed as many heads as I could.

We usually jump four or five times before Dad calls quits and cooks us a special dinner, white beans or spaghetti, so Mindy and I hike around the house for our second round. Mindy's halfway up the ladder and I've got one foot on the first rung, ready to go, when she holds a hand out behind her: *wait*. I back up to the chain link fence, where I can keep an eye on Dad and watch Mindy at the same time. Dad won't miss me for another few minutes, and then he'll only peer over the side of the trailer and holler at me to hurry my *be*-hind up before he has to come get me. Now he's looking peaceful, leaning on the roof like it's his throne and kingdom both, and we're so far from his mind you can almost see the memory of us dripping onto the aluminum.

Mindy steps close to the gutter, ponytail spilling out the back of her cap, and from the fence I can see the worn tips of her sneakers where she's written her name in red ink. She raises her arms, lowers her head, bends at the waist, and dives. Head-first, fingers pointed. I'm thinking, *Holy Mary, Mother of God*, but Mindy tucks her head expertly and continues all the way around, lands squat on her butt. She's done in a flash. I'm so excited I could spit turkeys because she did that—flipped!—but I know Dad's going to be furious. Mindy sits still for a moment, surprised or hurt I can't tell, then starts moving quickly: gets up, dusts her shorts, and walks away. Dad swings his legs over the side and drops down behind her, but instead of yelling at her, he looks at me and says, "Go on inside, Matt. Can't you see we're done?" Mindy veers off when she hears that, heads straight for the bathroom and sticks knives in the crack of the door, a trick she learned when she turned twelve and started taking baths again, so no one could get in, even if he knew how to pick the lock.

Dad takes his time wedging the ladder back into the shed, so I beat him inside and slide my fingers under the bathroom door to see if Mindy's okay. She tickles them, which means she is. Dad storms into the kitchen, throws open the freezer door and starts cracking trays of ice cubes, chucking them onto a dishrag. Then he sits at the table clutching the bundle, waiting until Mindy comes inching out like a stray cat, distrusting the air and everything in it.

"You fell pretty hard," he says, beckoning. "Let's see."

He pulls down her shorts enough to see the greening skin around her tail bone, which I don't notice as much as the pairs of yellow and purple underwear—extra padding—bunching up under her shorts. I look away because even though I've seen her underwear a million times, I'm not supposed to see this. Dad presses on Mindy's bruise like a doctor, and he asks if that hurts, but Mindy's clammed up tight as a stuck hinge. Dad pulls her shorts up and wheels her around to face him. I'm watching, but not directly. Not so she can see.

We stand there four loaded minutes, listening to Dad rock back and forth and waiting for him to explode. Finally, he bangs his fists so hard on the table that dust falls beneath it, then grips the edges. His face could kill birds. His knuckles are ashy. His hands are trembling, but it might be the wobbly table.

"Dammit, Mindy," he says. "What were you thinking?"

Dad wants more than anything to teach us how not to be brave, how to survive by the book, but Mindy—she's bold as a cold snap in July. She's got so much nerve it's dangerous.

"You could've broken your neck," Dad says. "You could've killed yourself."

But Mindy knows what she's doing. She picks up the dishrag and says, "May I?" and Dad shakes his head, shrugs. He doesn't even punish her. I follow her to our room and we climb to the top bunk with the blanket, leave the ice melting on the carpet. Mindy holds the science catalog above us and flips through the pages: instruments, dead animals for sale, fifty pages of scientific materials on recycled paper, a little box with a picture and price for each.

"We need cash," Mindy says, pointing at a black and white picture on page ten. "Look at this. Mail order. All we need's a COD and a stamp." The picture is of a cat fetus. You can't see the animal of it too well, but the shape is there, a curved sac of claws and eyelashes sealed in plastic, sold individually or by the case. Instructions printed on each bag.

"I'm going to get one of these," Mindy says. "A baby cat."

I try to concentrate on the magazine, but I'm wondering how she learned to flip without me even knowing.

"Mon-ey," Mindy says. "You got any ideas?"

"How'd you do it?" I say finally.

Mindy grins. She rubs her behind.

"Teach me," I say.

"Okay," Mindy says. "But we've got to get some money first."

"If I help you, will you teach me?" I say, and Mindy nods solemnly. If there's one thing she takes seriously, it's a deal.

I lie back, satisfied. Sure, I could probably learn to flip on my own, but then Mindy just might take off one day, leave me and Dad behind to hash it out alone. If the girl could flip off the roof, you just didn't know what else she might do. I didn't want that to happen. I wanted to be in on Mindy's plans. All of them. And if that meant supplying her with pickled cats until the day she died, well then, start the goddamn bidding.

We spend the next few weeks stockpiling tools: washed-out mason jars, empty vegetable cans, two paring knives and a zester, a jelly-bottomed pan, a bottle of amphibian saline solution. Pickers and pokers and squeezers. Things Mindy steals from school or I pull out of the trash. Then Dad finds a grocery bag full of stolen blue tweezers under the sink, and he starts going through

Mindy's belongings that night. You can tell he's suspicious that she's hiding more from him than what he can find. I show Mindy my secret spot under the trailer and she buries all the supplies back where the ground arches up to meet the kitchen floor. She ogles the pile of old crickets and says, "Been busy, huh?" I tell her about the ghosts, but she only laughs, tells me I take our game too seriously.

In fact, I don't hear the ghosts for three nights in a row, even though I can't sleep for all the listening I do. I think about sneaking out to find them, but decide against it—even crickets can have a taste for revenge. I try to force them out of hiding. I crush heads with an almost religious zeal. Twenty-five a day, sometimes. I keep count.

Dad starts on with the car wash place and with part of his bonus sends us out for double the usual lotto tickets. All of them are a bust but one, a High Roller, and Mindy cashes it to the delight of the woman behind the counter. It's only five bucks, but Mindy acts like she's under a spell the whole next week, coming home straight after school on the bus to leaf through her catalog and show me the lists of money-making schemes she's written on the backs of math dittos. McDonald's will hire fifteen-year-olds, she tells me, but I know she can't wait that long. Then I get my chance.

It starts with that idiot Tom Thornton calling me *white trash* in front of the whole class. I want to bash his face in, but I'm two strikes in the hole, so I keep my hands steady and pretty soon I'm quiet as a clear conscious. Everybody's watching to see what I'm going to do, including Tom himself, who looks like he just swallowed a bug and doesn't know how to get rid of it. Finally this creepy white kid who never talks, who only comes to class an hour at a time because he's slow or gifted or something, says to me, "Ten bucks for taking that asshole down." I don't like him, but Mindy and I take what we can get, and I figure it's Tom's own fault if he's made this many enemies. I nod, and at fifteen minutes to lunch I'm out the door with a bathroom pass. I make ready to whale on Tom like never before.

I'm not stupid, and I don't want to get suspended. But I've had a plan ever since these sixth graders got caught smoking on a ledge right over my classroom. My school is made of portables—one-room buildings they cart in on oversized flatbeds—connected by hallways that are always breaking apart, and these kids cracked part of the paneling so they could climb onto the roof. After they got caught, the janitor covered the hole with a screen, but it's so flimsy you could pry it off with a fingernail, which is what I do once I've shimmied up the hall post to the ledge. From here, I can slam Tom good and get out before anyone notices what's happened.

I hunker down and wait for Tom to come by, and he's last in line as usual. There's a nice, wide distance between him and the rest of the line. He's looking to the sides because he knows I'm somewhere waiting for him. He's thinking of bolting, I can tell. It's concrete down below, but that doesn't bother me a bit, and when Tom comes under me, I land on him like sixty-five pounds of pure hatred—smack. My ankle starts throbbing right away, but I get Tom pinned from behind and whisper, "You dipshit," in his ear. I twist his arm hard to let him know which one of us is trash.

When I try to run away—before anyone notices, just like I planned—Tom reaches around and grabs my throbbing ankle. I go down hard. I could make it still, could jump up and get out of there before word reaches the front of the line, but Tom looks at me with his drippy face, bleeding in all the right places, and he says it again, "White trash," and I get that soft-kneed feeling that means I'm going to lay into Tom's face until two different teachers are pulling me away, and all the alphabetical lines break free, and the kids throng around. My teacher orders me to stand to the side while he helps Tom, and I could run, but I know I'm doomed. I'm standing there, cursing myself, when I notice these guys staring at me. I say, "What's the deal?" and that makes most of them look away, all but the creepy kid who says, "You jump off the roof?" Tom's still gushing, and someone has come with paper towels so nobody's paying attention to me. I'm hyped up from the fight, so I say, "Yeah, so what?"

"Bullshit," the kid says, but he says it like he believes me. He digs out my money because he's a creep who keeps his word.

Since I'm getting suspended for ten measly bucks, I say, "Next time you're dishing out a hell of a lot more." The creep laughs.

"Next time," he says. "We'll see."

The principal calls my house, and Dad comes in looking deflated, saying he doesn't know what to do with me anymore, he didn't raise a fighting kid. The principal talks to Dad, then me, and then Dad repeats it all on the way home. It's not until we pull into our driveway that he finally stops talking. We sit there, buckled and locked in the car, and I watch a bee try to free itself from the windshield wiper. I'm looking at the bee when I see Mindy's backpack.

She isn't supposed to be home, but there it is, a blot of red in the secret spot. I can't see Mindy, but I know she's under there, fingernails digging. I wish I could believe she's just getting some extra tweezers or something, but I know in my stomach that she isn't retrieving. She's got something. An animal.

Without me.

The ten-dollar bill crumbles in my pocket. I look over at Dad, half-hoping he'll notice the backpack and investigate, but he's staring at the roof.

"My kids," he says, and he bows his head toward the steering wheel, rests it just clear of the horn. His voice is soft, his shoulders rounded like he's carrying the ladder.

"Oh, god," he says. "My kids."

Seeing my father like this, I am as close to confessing as I'll ever come. I want to rat out Mindy, blame it all on her. Instead I say, "I'm sorry, Dad. I didn't mean to."

He doesn't even turn his head in my direction.

Inside Dad washes the scrapes on my knuckles, turns my hands over and scrubs between my fingers and under the nails, until it starts to hurt and I pull away. I don't mention my ankle. It'll heal weak and a little off, always curving to the inside.

Mindy drifts through the back door like nothing's happening. "Hey," she says to me. "Caught again?"

"Shut up," I say.

Dad steps toward Mindy and then away. "What are you doing home?"

Mindy shrugs, tosses me a dishtowel. "Bomb threat. I got a ride."

"We'll see," Dad says, and heads for the phone. Mindy smiles prettily, hands clasped, which means her story will check out. A dark crust coats her nails, blacking out the pink decals she pasted there this morning. "Psst," she says when Dad's out of hearing range. "I have a surprise for you."

I glare at her. "I'm sick of surprises," I say.

"Wait'll you see it."

"I don't want to see it."

Mindy crosses her arms over her chest and leans to one side, looking off-balance. I put the ten on the table between us. When she reaches for it, I snatch it away.

She raises her eyebrows, then gives me a look I've seen her give Dad: lids narrowed, lip curled. "Fine," she says. "Keep your money. Give it to your *ghosts.*"

Then, quietly as water seeping out of the house, she slips across the linoleum. The kitchen floor stretches out long between us, almost too thin to support me and Mindy and Dad. Too fragile for our combined weight. One wrong step might send us crashing through to the thousands of cricket ghosts poised on hairy legs below.

I put the ten back on the table—I can't bring myself to keep it—and Dad picks it up when he's off the phone. He puts it in his pocket without a word. He looks out the door to where Mindy has gone, then at me. "Bomb threat," he says, like the words don't make sense.

I move closer to Dad when Mindy's gone. Like, for the moment, I understand exactly what he means.

Whatever Mindy does, it brings the crickets back. Maybe she chased them away in the first place, like a priest, with her buried box of tools. Or maybe this was the beginning of a handicap in sight—a hardening of the retina, a thickening of the heart—blips in my line of vision, like a TV station going in and out in a storm, right before the whole set goes blank.

That night, after Mindy and Dad fall asleep, I hear the crickets for the last time. They're everywhere: under the floor, at the window, on the roof. I step out of bed. I put on all my landing gear and point a flashlight out the kitchen window. The lawn is empty, safe to cross. I'm nervous the whole way from the kitchen to the secret spot, but the ghosts don't appear, not once, and it's weird, but the yard feels more frightening without them.

Once I get to the spot, I turn my back on the yard and shine the flashlight into the darkness under the house. There are the tools, and my piles of dead crickets. The light catches on a bed of foil in the corner, curled around something solid. I creep closer until I can see what's inside—an armadillo, maybe the most not-alive thing I've ever seen. Bashed up by a car, I can tell. Dead for hours, maybe days. What armor wasn't mauled by the car has been pared back and stacked next to the hairy body. With the butt of my flashlight, I flip the animal over and survey the other side where the wounds are slight, fine lines of torn flesh that look like healing scars. The eye is intact and open, guarding the armor beside it.

Armadillos are jumpers by instinct. I know this, having spooked them in the woods behind my school. It's pathetic, really, these left-over dinosaurs vaulting three feet in the air, toes spread, tails rigid, nostrils flared. Covered head to tail in armor. You see them all the time on the highway, pummeled and clawed apart, flung to the side of the road with legs splayed. Streams of road kill, a carcass for every mile marker.

And that's all this armadillo is—road kill. Staring at its remains in the beam of the flashlight, I realize I've been wrong. Mindy is no scientist. And neither, for that matter, am I.

What I cannot predict, in this moment, is how wrong I will turn out to be.

In a few months, my sister will bring a knife to school, but not for dissection. By the year's end, she'll have learned everything there is to know about skin, and the way it splits from the body like a renegade soldier.

Right now, all I know is that my sister has left me behind. But when I turn from the armadillo and switch off the light, I find that I'm not alone. There they are, the cricket ghosts, visible at last. So quiet that I didn't hear their arrival. Zinging across the yard and through the links in the fence. When I move, they flash blue and scatter, so I sit still on the edge of the lawn, let them grow brave enough to hurdle my legs. Their bodies are smooth, sightless, but they seem to know where they're going. They have a sense of the yard. They could escape it if they wanted. When I put out my hand, they slide through the skin, and in the instant they pass I can see what's inside my fist: blood working through veins, tendons and bones and cartilage and fat. Everything hot and pulsing for a minute before the cricket drops out and my hand goes dark. I hear a noise behind me, and when I turn I see the armadillo, up and nosing through the dirt, snuffling at its piled armor. Gripping the earth; holding it. I'm happy for it, and happy that I can stay out here where things go on. I tell myself that Mindy must be in the business of making ghosts, too. That maybe we have that in common.

Later, back in bed and trying to sleep, the image of Tom Thornton will slip into my head. The colors: the deep brown of his skin, the lesser brown of the drying blood, the white of the paper towels. The brilliance of the new blood, thick and oxygen-rich, bolder than me or Tom or any of the boys sweating in the shade of the hallway. Liquid, pulsing up and out of its veins, and—in the moment my teacher takes the paper towel away, just before the blood hits the concrete—alive and naked, flying. I'll want to hit Tom again, and again, and again, just to see it.

as human as you are
standing here

❦

The one time we slept together, I called my friend Leo an experiment. He'd just lost the last Mama Guava drag contest at El Goya, an abandoned cigar factory turned nightclub in Ybor City, and I was trying to console him. We were on a brick parking lot, no lights or cops, and both of us were wearing skirts which, physically anyway, made things easier. I straddled Leo's hips, he held onto my knees.

Look, Leo said beneath me. I'm a lesbian.

He laughed, still thinking I was joking. A blonde wig slid back from his forehead. Behind us, El Goya shut down forever. Leo placed my hand like a corsage on his chest, and I pushed into him.

Gyp, he said. What are you doing?

Nothing, I said. Then I did it again.

Leo turned so he was looking at the tire of the car parked next to us. I noticed one of his false eyelashes had separated from the corner of his eye.

Okay, he said. But go slow. Go slow.

It's just an experiment, I said before we both stopped talking.

A week later, he showed up at my apartment in a blue Chevy Cavalier I'd never seen, wearing a French push-up bra that I couldn't stop staring at. He'd only been 'moning—using hormones—for a couple weeks, but in that bra he sure had some Mademoiselles. He went straight to my closet and pulled out two shirts, a low-cut number someone had bought for me and another with fringe. He told me he was taking them.

Taking them where? I said.

West, he said, shrugging, like it was just another club. He raised the shirts in his fist, proclamation-like.

I'm jetting, Gyp, he said. I just can't *live* in a place where sodomy is still on the books.

Sodomy, I said, and I might've even laughed. Give me a break.

He glared at me. Huffed. Maybe not this one, he said, handing me back the shirt with fringe.

He did leave Florida, though, drove all the way to Colorado and moved into the slums, sent me pictures through the mail like postcards: his skinny arm wrapped around boy after boy after boy. I guessed the boys were supposed to prove something, but I knew he'd be back. It was just a matter of waiting, of riding out his absence like a jail sentence. I sent quarter postcards to his return addresses, the gag tourist kind with obese people and alligators and bad puns. Send money, I wrote on the backs, as a joke. *When you come home, bring flowers.*

With Leo gone, I started working more hours at Sunflower Organics, ringing up rainforest-friendly shampoo and tempeh burgers, herbs for migraines and weight loss and incontinence. I put in so many hours the other clerks made jokes about where I must be spending the night. I didn't mention Leo, except to refer casually to a friend I had out West. Sure, *theoretically* being a twenty-first-century queer meant you fucked whom you pleased. *Theoretically,* banging a drag queen was cutting edge. But when it came down to the blow-by-blow of daily life, people in health food stores wanted to know where you stood. And while sleeping with him didn't exactly make me straight, it put me somewhere closer to the middle. So, I let my coworkers set me up with their roommates and cousins and neighbors, a lot of nice-enough dykes who just weren't Leo. And I spent a lot of time having imaginary confrontations with people who didn't ask the right questions. Who said a lesbian and a drag queen couldn't fall in love, shack up in a townhouse with white shutters, a couple of fish, and a couple of incomes?

Who said?

And anyway, theory couldn't erase the sound of Leo's voice— *Go slow, go slow*—so when I wasn't working, I skulked around bars where, if I was lucky, I could find political affirmation in some poor dyke's crotch. And where I could ignore the fact that there was nothing political about the way I missed Leo.

Then, a year after he'd traded me for the road, I got a letter on wide-ruled paper with a Statue of Liberty stamp that said, *I'm in jail and all I want to do is shoot every one of these motherfuckers in the face*, and I knew he was coming back.

He turned up on my doorstep with a ring through his bottom lip and an ugly patchwork of stitches across his right cheek. He grinned when I opened the door, all tongue because he'd lost his front teeth, wearing lipstick and a Buccaneers ball cap. The cap, in case he got pulled over by some fag-hating cop. The lipstick, like ointment on a wound.

I'm out, Gyp, he said, and I knew he meant Colorado, not jail. He'd been busted for forging prescriptions, then for slugging the arresting officer. Leo wasn't a large person, but he did have a long history of beating the shit out of people. It was one of the many things we had in common.

I mean, I'm home, Leo said. I hugged him. I could feel the flat edges of his shoulder blades through his shirt, the knots of his spine. His hair was stiff and smelled like gasoline. He could've been a public service announcement for himself. I wanted to peel off his clothes and count the pieces of him to make sure he was all there.

Leo, I said finally. Holy shit.

Straight boys, he said. They'll be the death of me.

They'll be the death of us all, I said.

Except you, Leo said.

Why, I said. Because I sleep with queens?

Leo didn't say anything.

You come back just to stick it to me? I said.

He stepped forward, closer to me, over the threshold of my door. He said, I came back because I love you.

Which wasn't true. I knew he came because he had nowhere else to go. Because straight boys in Florida or Colorado or anywhere else were never as nice as you hoped they'd be, and neither, for that matter, were gay ones. Because I'd been taking him in since tenth grade, when his parents kicked him out and I let him crash in my room until I got kicked out, too. Because I was the only person who knew that even when he was being mean and catty and predictable, he was still Leo, my Leo, and that counted for something. And because what else could I do when he batted his eyes and called me Gypsy—his pet name for me when we'd lived on the street—but step aside and let him in.

He collapsed on my couch for three days before getting up again. The first night, I asked him about the lip ring, and he said it was a Neptune figure that symbolized humanity's alienation from itself. I asked about the stitches, and he winced. They were from when he'd gotten slow drunk in a straight bar, he said, in Evergreen. He'd driven his pickup over the side of Holy Shit Road, which ran in gravel switchbacks up the mountainside. He didn't say what he'd been doing there all alone, or who had rescued him, or if he'd meant to go over the edge or not.

I told him about Sunflower Organics, and the bars, and the postcards I'd sent that he'd never gotten. I kept touching his knees, his elbows. The parts of him that seemed safe.

By the third night, I'd cancelled all my dates and called in sick twice. Leo barely got up to eat. He slept a lot, but he wasn't going through withdrawals, so I didn't think he'd been on anything but the hormones. The third day, my boss Steve called. Leo woke up enough to ask who it was, as if he'd been expecting a call himself.

Nobody, I said. Have you seen my keys?

I put on my orange Sunflower smock, and when he finally opened his eyes, Leo looked startled.

I'm going to work, I said. When he didn't respond, I repeated, My keys?

I took them last night, Leo said. He reached between the couch cushions and pulled out the plastic keychain.

You went out? I said.

Leo grinned, flashing a new set of false teeth. They were too white, and a bit too long for his face.

Without me? I said.

You looked so cute, Leo said. I couldn't wake you.

Where'd you get the teeth?

The Tooth Fairy, he said.

Leo.

What? he said, dropping his eyes.

Leo insisted on coming with me to work, but refused to change out of his pajamas—my flannel pants, a sleeveless shirt, and flip flops. At Sunflower, he headed straight for the herbal remedies and then set up a battalion of over-the-counter drugs at my register. Saw Palmetto, Black Cohosh, Mexican Yam, Tansy. Hops and Dong Quai. He ran his tongue over his new teeth, clicked his lip ring against them.

What are all these? I said.

Two for my titties, he said, lifting the bottles. Two for curves. One for a creamy complexion. And one—he sighed—to take away my sex drive. How do you stand it?

Baby, that's a lot of meds, I said.

They're not *meds*, he said. They're vitamins.

He looked over his shoulder at the only other clerk, working in the free-range deli. He said, Are there cameras in here?

No, I said. Healthy people don't steal.

Beautiful, he said. He reached across the scanner and grabbed a plastic bag. He loaded it with bottles.

Keep the receipt, he said. I'll walk home.

Stealing's a bad habit, I said. I watched the other clerk, behind the meat counter, set out the happy carcasses of free-range rabbits. The automatic doors slid open and a hippy couple walked in, openly stared at Leo.

Pay for it, then, Leo said. Fix me.

He smiled like he might be joking, and the smile reminded me that Leo had lived for a long time without money. That he had a habit of stealing things he couldn't buy, and offering things he couldn't afford to give.

Pay with what? I said.

Leo put the back of his hand to his forehead, a mock-swoon. This proves it, he drawled. I cannot be fixed.

Then he strutted out the automatic door.

After he was gone, I found copies of all the bottles he'd walked out with. I rang them up and put money in the drawer.

Once he'd gotten out of bed, Leo stayed away more and more. He returned long enough to tell me about the other trannies he'd met, DQ girls with implants, non-ops with shaved tracheas, genderfucks who refused to get cut. I answered calls for Leona, Leonora, and, once, Leontyne. One night he fell in the door, pumped full of silicone, and when I asked how he'd gotten it, he pulled down the waistband of his pants.

The usual way, he said. In the ass.

He peeled back a bandage, and the wound was purple and swollen. There were several visible needle marks. Someone hadn't known what they were doing.

I meant, how'd you pay for it, I said.

Oh, you know, Leo said, waving me away. Sugar and spice and everything nice.

I didn't mind gore, and I'd broken enough skin to be immune to the sight of blood. But those little needle pricks bothered me. Leo had messed up his body so bad it didn't want to heal: the wounds on his face had begun to weep. Now those holes suggested that the damage was working its way inside-out.

I said the only thing I thought would get to him. Leo, I said. It's not pretty.

He replaced the bandage quickly. Patience, dear, he said. I'm still cooking. I'm not done yet.

I'm not buying you any more drugs, I said.

Leo pulled up his pants. I didn't ask you to.

You could help out, I said. Do a dish, for god's sake. Wash a sock.

Your vein sticks out when you're mad, Leo said, tapping his forehead. I have a friend who could take care of that.

That night, he didn't come home.

When he did return, the next day, Leo brought me socks. A brand new pair. I laughed. From then on, he brought gifts every time he came home. Little things at first: a Patchouli-scented candle, a mood toe ring, a collection of lesbian erotica I already owned.

I've read it, I said when he handed me the book.

Leo raised two perfectly plucked eyebrows. Gypsy, he said. Go girl.

After that the presents got bigger, more dangerous. He brought home two hits of speed that we took for old time's sake. We spent the night giving each other peanut-butter-and-jelly facials, and I called everyone in my phone book to tell them they were mean drunks and hang up. Leo left me writing furiously on my bathroom wall, and when he returned, it was with a small aquarium he set down in my living room. By the time I emerged from the bathroom, the tank was already lit and bubbling at the surface, a plastic treasure chest spilling gold coins on the bottom. Fake seaweed swayed with the current, and some sort of algae sprouted near the top. There were no fish, but that wasn't surprising. I figured it was just like Leo to bring home an aquarium stocked with everything but the point. But just when I thought I'd pegged Leo, I noticed something moving on the bottom. I squinted, then got down on all fours and peered inside.

What the fuck is that? I said. What the *fuck* is that?

Settle down, Leo said calmly. I'm just babysitting.

That's not a baby, I said. Is it alive?

Yes. And it is so a baby.

Leo got up, plunged a hand into the tank, and with two blood red fingernails, withdrew a miniature alligator. Only about ten inches long, the body lashed back and forth until Leo flipped it over and stroked the pale underside.

See, he said, she's harmless. A pet, like a dog. My friend got her at a fruit stand in Louisiana.

I don't like dogs, I said.

I waited for the gator to open its reptilian jaws and latch onto Leo's finger. The black eyes didn't move, and its tiny teeth curled over its snout. I shuddered.

How long?

Just for the weekend, Leo said. Want me to put her back?

Leo got up and slid the gator off his palm into the aquarium, where it floated with feet splayed. Body submerged up to the eyes. Louisiana's best. In my living room. In an aquarium with no lid.

Can't it get out? I said.

Leo laughed. What, crawl up the glass? It's not an insect. It's like a fish, Gyp, a big fish with legs. Just for the weekend.

Fish don't have legs, I said.

And as thanks—Leo went over to the counter and held up a syringe—I got this.

Heroin? I said.

Premarin, Leo said. The real stuff.

That night, while the alligator floated in fake seaweed, I shot Leo full of hormones. He hadn't had any in a week, so I figured it would be okay. He wanted me to do it directly in the boob, but I refused—I knew enough about 'moning to know that you could O.D. by shooting up in the wrong place. I told Leo to give me his ass, and he did, and then I had to look at all his bruises. He'd been stuck so many times that the skin had dimpled. I chose the least marked place and pressed in the needle. Leo exhaled. I half expected him to murmur, *Go slow, go slow.*

Afterward—after he'd pulled up his pants and hugged me with wet eyes: You're my girl, he'd said—he wanted to take a bubble bath. Even more, he wanted me to cut out his stitches.

What am I, your nurse? I said.

Come on, he said. Help me. I don't trust anyone else.

So I did. I used nail scissors to strip away surgical thread and dried bits of old blood, while Leo snuggled under a blanket of raspberry bubbles and tried not to flinch. I felt good, like I was snipping away all the dead layers of the past two years. I rinsed the scissors in his bath water, letting my hand slip close to the space where his body lay. Leo didn't open his eyes. When I was done, his cheek looked only a little less gory.

That's the best I can do, I said.

Eyes still closed, chin resting in foam, Leo said, Thank you, baby. He raised one hand out of the water, cutting a hole in the wall of bubbles, and felt the side of his face.

I told you I went over the side of Holy Shit Road, right? he said.

You told me, I said.

And you believed me, right? he said.

I don't believe anything you tell me, Leo, I said. I sighed, because I knew what was coming. Leo held up his hand to quiet me.

I'm trying to confess, he said.

A boyfriend would've been a respectable way to get hit, he told me. All the trannies had stories about violent homophobes they'd taken shit from in the name of love; they all had thin scars they covered with foundation. Those were stories you told your girls over late night tequila shots. But Leo's mangled cheek was not because of a boyfriend. It was over another girl. Like him. And that was the kind of story you didn't tell anyone.

It was some chick who had the hots for me, he said. A total brick—five o'clock shadow and everything. She wasn't ugly, but she wasn't—he paused, licking his lip ring—pretty. She came onto me in this bar, and I don't know what happened. I was on some bad shit, I think. She made a move and I told her to fuck off, but she wouldn't leave.

Leo looked up at me, took my hand and held it. He smiled, but he'd taken out his teeth, and without them the gesture seemed off.

I beat her up, he said. Bad. Some of the boys pulled me off and messed up my face outside. Then I drove up to Holy Shit Road and sat there for hours with the motor running. Bled all over the steering wheel.

I stroked his hair, which was thinning even though he was barely in his twenties. He looked like a little old lady in his tower of bubbles, two hairless, bony knees resting against the sides of the tub. He looked like he wanted to end the story there, but I knew that the key to keeping Leo was to keep him talking.

What was it that made you so mad? I said.

Her mouth, Leo said. And her hair. The way she smelled. She was just so sad. And she didn't have to be that sad, you know? She could've tried harder.

He turned his head toward the wall. She was a disgrace to the profession, he said.

She didn't deserve it, I said.

I know. But I got mine, didn't I?

I couldn't disagree. It was hard to feel like he hadn't made up for it—in pain, in humiliation. He'd spent his whole life making up for the things he was going to do later. His punishment preceded his crimes.

I woke up ten minutes and three days late for work.

Don't go, Leo said as I splashed water from the kitchen sink on my face, splattering my Sunflower uniform.

I'll get fired if I don't, I said.

Then you could come out with us more, Leo said.

Truthfully, I thought I'd be fired anyway. Steve had already warned me. He wasn't going to overlook one more late arrival, one more no show. Even hippies had their limits.

But when I showed up at Sunflower, no one even noticed. They were all in the back, crowded around a black-and-white TV Steve kept there for, he said, emergencies. I clocked in silently.

When I joined the rest of them in the back, they barely noticed my presence.

Protest weekend, one of the workers, a pregnant woman named Lisa, murmured over her shoulder.

What protest? I said.

Some security system in Ybor. Visionics. It's all over the news. She paused to look at me meaningfully. The *national* news, she said.

Ybor City was fifteen minutes away from Tampa proper, the heavily hair-sprayed newscaster was saying, and bordered housing developments on one side and the Tampa tourist strip on the other. That made for lots of crime, so to combat its bad reputation, the Ybor City Council had hired a company called Visionics to install scanners on public streets. Face scanners. Walk down the street, the newscaster pronounced, and a computer would compare your face to a database of America's Most Wanted.

Innocent until scanned, Steve-the-free-range-butcher said. Screw that.

Legalized profiling, another worker said, shaking his head.

And now they've got technology on their side, Steve said. They don't even need a real reason to arrest somebody.

It's just wrong, Lisa said. Somebody should do something.

I knew what was coming before Steve said a word. In an organic food store, *somebody should do something* is as good as a call to action. Steve agreed to close shop early so we could go to the protest.

Wear a disguise, he told us all. Don't let them see your face.

I went home and told Leo, who nodded solemnly.

Ybor City, he said. You can't trust anything there.

He was cycling, and this was his week off hormones. I'll be moody like you, he'd told me earlier, and I'd said, What's new? Leo agreed to come with me anyway, and together we went to the store for costume makeup—fake blood and face paint and latex bullet wounds you could stick to your skin. This last item was Leo's choice.

By the way, I said on the way home. El Goya's gone.

Good riddance.

It's called the Pleasure Dome now. It's only gay on Tuesdays.

What about drag shows? Leo said.

It's not the same, I said. It's nothing like it used to be.

The truth was, the Pleasure Dome still had drag shows, but they were peopled by tourists now, middle-aged straight couples drinking mai tais and gaping at the "he-shes." At the old El Goya, Leo and I had drunk key lime martinis until the key lime ran out and we'd switched to straight vodka. I'd watched Leo belt out a version of "Mississippi Goddam" that would've done Nina Simone proud. I'd left him dancing with a glass propped against one thigh and a trailer trash homo rubbing on the other. And one night, I'd consoled him on a brick parking lot, no lights or cops.

Shit, Leo said. It never used to be much.

Leo did my makeup for the evening protest: a kind of Halloween-style drag, with green face paint, black circles around my eyes, fake blood at my temples and in the middle of my forehead. War veteran, he pronounced. For himself, he used latex. He layered himself in standard drag queen makeup—thick eyelashes, cherry red lipstick, rouge, and shadow. Then he affixed the bullet holes to his neck and cleavage. He wore a white plastic mini and a halter.

Look at me, I said when I looked in the mirror. You made me look hideous.

You? Leo said. Look at my poor face.

He frowned at his cheek, which had scabbed over since I cut the stitches out, and he rubbed another dose of foundation into the red and pink slashes. Nothing to be done, he said. I'm scarred.

You can hardly tell, I told him. I think they're shrinking.

I think they're growing, Leo said. I think they're breeding.

We decided to start the evening with a drag show at the old El Goya Showroom in the Pleasure Dome. I figured we'd spend half an hour laughing at the Cher knock-offs in stonewashed jeans before zipping over to meet the Sunflower gang, thereby saving my job and my ass. Sure, there was a little part of me that wanted to revisit the crime scene, relive the events that had made, one night, me and Leo think we had answers for each other. But more than that, after what Leo had confessed to me in the tub, I wanted him to remember that some chick in Colorado was not the only offense he needed to atone for.

Ybor City was always crowded, but that night it was packed. Turned out all of Tampa was up in arms about the scanners, and everybody was talking about should we or shouldn't we—surveil, that is. People weren't so much dressed in costume as they were disguising themselves. Nobody had a face: only bags, hats, and dark glasses. To the right of us, a Canadian Air Force gas mask; to the left, a Ronald Regan pull-on. There were a couple of Lone Rangers, lots of ski masks. Leo grabbed my hand, told me not to stare at the straight people.

On Twelfth Street, a guy wearing a sign that advertised free Jello shots was handing out bandannas and yelling, Fuck Visionics.

Fuck who? Leo asked him.

You know, the guy said, gesturing vaguely at the buildings. The cameras.

Leo took a blue bandanna; I took a red. We tied them around our faces up to the eyes. With his face covered like that, Leo's eyes looked enormous: the red glitter on his lids sparkled and made his pupils look deep as his gunshot wounds.

All we need's a couple of pistols and holsters, Leo said. I even *have* holsters.

We edged our way up the street, jostling against people who smelled like leather and plastic, like makeup that was beginning to melt in the heat. We paid two bucks apiece to get bar codes drawn on our faces by a painter wearing a red bandanna and a T-shirt that said, Digitize This! She normally drew caricatures at Busch Gardens, she said, but she'd come out tonight in support of free speech.

Free speech? I said, holding my head still while she drew on my cheek with a black crayon.

Our right to privacy, she said. To walk down the street without being part of a national line-up.

During Leo's turn, she accidentally smeared the crayon across his forehead. Leo pushed her hand away.

Relax, I said to him. It's fine.

Fix it, he demanded. I didn't want any trouble that night, so I took the crayon from the woman and did it myself.

Leo held my hand even as the crowd thickened and we had to shove our way through. He skipped through the entrance of the Dome like it was nothing, paused only briefly to take in the name of the El Goya Showroom. Under the black lights, his white skirt eclipsed the rest of him, turned him into a walking, talking ass. On the stage, a big queen with implants was warming up the crowd in the kind of hot pants that made believers out of straight men. She had a good thirty-eight inches of leg plus platforms, stockings patterned with silhouettes: reclining nudes, men and women both.

Where do you put it? someone yelled.

The queen looked down at her crotch, back at the crowd. Honey, she said, I've been fucking my liver for five hours.

Leo shook his head as we entered. He waved away the performer—Old girls, old jokes, he said—and went to order a martini from the bare-chested bartender.

The first performer sang Madonna and the second—predictably—sang Cher. Leo rolled his eyes, whispered to me that drag shows were all top-forty medleys these days, watered-down hip hop and rap, maybe some R & B thrown in for diversity. Whatever overdeveloped pre-teens were singing on MTV, Leo said, these thirtysomething trannies were lip-synching at the Dome. Back at the El Goya, it'd been all Ella Fitzgerald and Aretha Franklin, and did I remember when he'd sung that Nina Simone song?

God help me if I ever start singing Cher, he said.

You were good, I said.

I still am.

Leo downed four martinis in half an hour, and then he started heckling the performers. Where are the real girls? he yelled. Where are all the pretty young things? When he ordered the fifth martini, the bartender looked at me. I told Leo we needed to talk. I dragged him into a stall in the women's bathroom and locked the door. I'd had several martinis myself, and every time Leo looked at me with those gunshot eyes, I felt like I was falling. In the stall, we took off our bandannas with an urgency we might've, under other circumstances, removed our clothes. Leo slouched on the seat, eyes half-closed.

I love you, Gypsy, he said.

How long are you back for, Leo?

Don't call me Leo, he said. He opened his eyes. He said, It's not pretty.

How long?

Gypsy, he said. I want to go on stage.

A couple of weeks? I said. Longer? I shook his shoulders, like it mattered what he might say. Like if I shook him hard enough, he might say, I'm staying forever, Gyp, just for you. And what would that mean? The white townhouse? I couldn't justify my attraction to him forever by saying he looked better in a dress than me. I couldn't even justify Leo to my coworkers. Whenever they'd asked, I'd said Leo was a cousin. He'd fallen on hard times, I'd said. He needed a friend.

When I stopped shaking Leo's shoulders, his head flopped forward onto his chest.

I could've never left *you*, I said.

His head snapped up so quickly I wondered how much of the drunkenness he'd been faking.

You've been waiting a long time to say that, he said. Feel better?

No, I said. Not at all.

I'm going up. On stage.

You want to go up, I said, then go up.

He clasped my hands. You'll wait?

Twenty minutes, I said. Then I have to meet the people from my work.

Oh, the hippies, he said. The big, fat hippies. They'll live.

He left the stall first, then me. I flushed the toilet, though we hadn't used it. I washed my hands, held them under the hot air dryer long after they'd dried. I supposed I should start calling him Leona or Leonora. Or L, like some of his other friends did. I supposed I should start referring to him in the feminine.

I supposed I'd lost his respect because I hadn't realized that earlier.

Leo took over during the finale. He walked onto the stage with his neck full of bullet holes, and one by one, he made fun of the other performers, swaying a little on his feet and pausing to sip from an empty martini glass. The Madonna look-alike tried to shoo him away, but he ridiculed her so thoroughly she seemed close to tears.

Now, Madonna, he said. There's a fucking hard imitation. You learn to lip sync when you were sucking cock, honey?

When Madonna had gone, Leo began to sing. No introduction, no accompaniment. Just Leo, crooning, wooing, melting onto the stage. His skirt was so bright it hurt my eyes.

Got a moon above me, he whispered, but no one to love me. Lover man, oh, where can you be?

When he walked off the stage, he was crying.

We left immediately. Leo, I think, suspected trouble. I just wanted to get to Steve and Lisa and the rest of the people who understood how not-crazy I was, to be in the dark, hidden, disguised as somebody else. But the girls from the Dome were faster than us. And Leo had more coming to him than even I could've predicted.

Maybe they didn't mean to hurt him. I couldn't imagine why they cared about a skinny, battered kid who'd managed to humiliate himself much more than he'd shamed them. Maybe they just wanted to dissolve him a little, kill some of that cockiness with a couple of snide remarks. They didn't realize that Leo was on a suicide mission that night. And this wasn't going to be another Holy Shit Road—this time, he wasn't going to let them let him get away.

There they were when we stepped outside, five of them, charcoal-eyed and larger than life. Leo didn't even try to run.

Nice face, the Madonna said pointing at Leo's scars with her eyes. You get that from your boyfriend?

Meaning me. I almost laughed. I would've, had these girls not been towering over Leo. He brushed his skirt, wiped his bottom lip. He glanced at me, and I willed him to stay calm. I watched his hands. The Madonna touched his cheek, and he smacked her hand away. She grinned, and the other girls circled.

Fuck off, I said. Leave him alone.

Leo blinked. I winced. The girls—every one—raised their penciled eyebrows, smiled at each other.

Him? a biker chick said to Leo. So what are you, honey? You a man? You just a dick in a skirt? Aw, honey, she said, are you just confused?

Leo looked back at me, and I shook my head. The Pleasure Dome began thumping with late night disco music. On the street, a police car cruised by.

I'm sorry, Leo said to me. And still looking at me, he hauled off and punched the biker chick so hard that she fell backward. Her head hit the sidewalk with a loud crack.

Oh, Leo, I said. Then I leapt at Madonna, cut my knuckles on her teeth. I did my best to fend off four of them, while Leo kept hitting the one on the ground. He kneeled, and hit, and said with each punch, Human. I'm human, that's what. As fucking human as you are standing here.

They broke open Leo's stitches, pushed his nose closer to the right side of his face. Ripped his clothes. Leo just curled into a ball. I was raging, all over the place, bobbing and weaving through three at once, adrenaline pumping straight through to my fists. For every hit I took, I claimed a body part for Leo: a tooth, a rib, a tittie. They were decent fighters, but I had love on my side. At least, that was what I kept telling myself while Leo was curled into that ball. I had Leo on my side.

It all ended when one of the bouncers came outside for a smoke. Hey, he yelled, and that startled me back into awareness. The bouncer ran to where the biker chick was lying on the ground, Leo still beside her. I had lacerations along my palms and wrists, scratches down my neck, and blood streaming from somewhere on my face, but I managed to drag Leo to standing. His lip was severed where the ring had been. One of his breasts, small as a pre-teen girl's, had flopped out of his shirt. Blood collected in the bullet holes on his neck and around his eyes. A few of his false teeth were stuck to his shirt.

Instinctively, I looked up. Wondering where the reflective circles were, the bluish eyes adjusting, focusing, fixing us in a computerized memory. I knew we were doomed, but I didn't want to end up in the back of a patrol car just yet. Me and Leo, we still had stuff to talk about.

Gyp, he slurred, we've got to go.

I knew without asking why he needed to leave, just as the day he'd turned up on my doorstep, I hadn't needed to see bruises to know where he was black and blue.

I helped Leo back to the Centro Ybor parking lot, and piled all the gangly legs of him into the car. I asked if he needed the hospital, but he said no, and since I couldn't afford it anyway, we went home. I told him I'd fix him up at my place. I said everything would be okay.

Leo rolled his head onto my shoulder, wiped his nose on my jacket.

What about the hippies? he said.

I don't know, I said. We'll figure something out.

It's all my fault.

I know.

Leo burbled a laugh. Bitch, he said.

He looked out the window, traced a slick finger against the glass. You'd beat up everybody for me, wouldn't you? he said. I think you'd even beat up me for me.

I'd never hit you, I said quickly.

Same difference, Leo said. Right? I saw you wailing on those girls. I saw your face. You liked it.

I stared straight ahead, my eyes fixed on the wavering white lines in front of me. I was helping your ass out, I said. Then, after a moment, Maybe I liked that part a little.

Oh, Leo said. Then he shook his head and straightened up. No, he said. That's weird. I mean, that's just sad.

He wiggled around in his seat so he was facing me, all bruised skin and torn clothes. He patted his chest with his fingers, delicate.

I know what am I, Leo said. I'm not the one who's confused. But you—what are you, Gyp? You gay? Straight?

He threw his arm out, hit the window. I concentrated on steering, telling myself that to keep Leo was to keep him talking. And at that moment, I desperately wanted him to shut up.

You're the one who's confused, Leo said again. Not me. You're the one too scared to admit you want dick.

I didn't say anything, and eventually Leo slumped against the window and began to weep.

Not dick, Leo, I thought.

I had to carry him up the stairs. When I opened the door, everything seemed wrong, as if someone had broken in, though all my things were in place. The light was too big, and the walls were too tall, and the room was too wide to cross. I felt like there were eyes on me. I knew it was only a matter of time before someone knocked on my door; it wouldn't take long for Visionics to find a match for my face. I hadn't been in trouble in a long time, but I knew the past was there, waiting for some electronic memory to find it.

We shouldn't be here, I said. We have to leave.

But Leo was frozen, ear cocked to the ceiling. I listened, too, and from somewhere deep inside my apartment, I heard a grunting.

Jesus, I said. That sounds like the gator.

The aquarium bubbled thirstily from the floor, reflecting light onto the wall. Lidless. Empty. For a moment, its hollow bubbling was the only sound. Then, again—a couple of prolonged grunts, like someone trying to start a car.

Leo limped across the room, a hand to his ear. When he turned, his delight showed so plainly through the grotesque wounds that to look at him made my skin hurt.

You need peroxide, I said. I had it, as well as all kinds of other pills and ointments and salves. But I didn't move to get any of it.

She's calling to us, he said. She's lost. She thinks we're other alligators.

When I didn't follow him at first, he stamped his foot. Help me, he said.

It took us a few minutes to determine that the noise was coming from the bedroom. I stopped listening for police at the door, started listening for the baby gator. We put our ears next to the bed, in the closet, by the night stand. We shined a flashlight under the dresser, and Leo prodded shadows with a coat hanger. We closed our eyes and tried to think reptilian. Still the gator eluded us; its plaintive noises seemed to come directly from the walls.

When I left the room, Leo was tapping the wall with one finger—*da dum, da dum,* like a heartbeat. His cheek, when he leaned in to listen, left a blood print on the white paint.

Don't leave yet, he said. We're getting closer. I can feel it.

the *niña*, the *pinta*, the *santa maria*

∞

I f you stick out your thumb, a car might stop, and then what will you do?

Then what?

Here's your answer: walk. Keep walking. Past the apartment of the woman with long earrings who is leaning over a liter can of beer and laughing a sound like exhaustion. Past the crazy man at the bus stop, and the fat lady with braids explaining to him that she doesn't give a good god *damn* about the *Niña*, the *Pinta*, or the *Santa Maria*. Repeat her words after you pass. Good god *damn*. Good god *damn*.

This is what you'll say to the car, should it stop.

To yourself, say you were just trying to catch, on the whirl of your thumb, one of the stout, wet snowflakes that have been

falling here all spring, and falling, too, ever since you smirked
and took the long way home, the one your mother warned you
for the last time not to take, down through the rocks in the
ravine, where you lost your keys. Which is exactly what she said
you'd do. It snowed through your search, your retracing of
steps, and it's snowing now as you walk down Indianola Street
toward the bar where you hope your mother will be. It should
be rain, this snow—it melts upon contact and leaves splash
marks on your jeans—but the flakes cling to frost like it's
promised them something.

It's dark, and the snow has whipped your hair and swabbed
out your ears, but you have only to walk, and you don't need your
hair and ears for that. Ahead, somewhere in the swirling distance,
is a bar with a marquee low enough to smack, and lights just dim
enough for people to rise from their stools and begin to dance.
Your mother will be there, you hope, but you won't tell her about
the ravine, or how you pressed yourself into the rocks like they
were another person holding you. You won't say anything about
your missing keys. You'll ask for her spare set, or maybe you'll just
lift the keychain from her back pocket, unnoticed, quiet as hope.

So, walk. Keep walking—past a group of men in paint-
splattered jeans smoking on a porch, their cigarettes glowing
like heart monitors. Past a stray dog trailing a busted chain. The
people on the porch and the dog look at you the same way: like
you are a prize they didn't win. Past the Dairy Queen cup filled
with unmelted ice cream, left in the gutter as if just five minutes
ago someone became fed up with ice cream and snow and all of
Ohio and went in search of better things. That's what you'd like
to do: hitch a ride out of town, or at least to the bar. You imagine
treasure maps, cities of gold, coral chips washing up like pieces of
the same puzzle. Three ships in the distance toss their sails like
manes, and you know they're thinking that you—your stringy
hair, your too-tight jeans—aren't exactly who they wanted to see.

Put your thumbs away. There's nobody on Indianola Street going to take you anywhere good.

Anyway, hasn't a car already stopped?

Don't turn around to look at it. Don't. Feel the kill of the engine in your chest, the breath of brakes on your neck, the turning of tires in the ground under your feet. Is it really happening? Has this car really stopped for you?

You bet your good god *damn* it has.

And if you were in a different kind of place, where the blue plastic baby swing you are passing wasn't hanging askew on the rotting porch, and where the porch, after all, wasn't rotting, then you might just swing your hips and laugh at the car, or grin and get in. If it hadn't just passed your eleven o'clock curfew, which you know because the traffic light started flashing yellow in time with your stride, then you might not need to duck down an alley and run toward a busted chain fence, behind which a man and a cigarette are barbequing something raw.

But as it is, you aren't anywhere else. You—your mouth, your fingers, your truant thumb—are what the man is barbequing. Even as you hide, crouched behind a dumpster, you have the feeling that this is the start of your body parts getting the better of you.

Catch your breath; the car is still somewhere behind you on Indianola Street. You know this street, though nothing, now, looks familiar. Inhale. Exhale. Say it out loud: *I don't give a good god* damn *about the* Niña, *the* Pinta, *or the* Santa Maria. Consider, from now on, telling people that Niña is your street name. Decide that if you do get into the car, that's what you'll say.

The sound of tires crunching gravel brings you back. The car inches along until it is past the alley. Heads hang out the windows, looking. It could be your mother, furious with you, inside. It could be someone lost. Creep out once the car is gone. Walk back to the street. The pride of getting away, the disappointment—it feels as if they've gotten under your thumbnail.

Screw the bar. Your mother isn't there, anyway. She's somewhere else, unzipping things, undoing things. This is how people lose each other. They find themselves in the wrong place, calling things by the wrong name.

You can see the street sign from here. You are not on Indianola Street at all.

Walk backward toward a locust tree. Toward the painters on the porch. "Hey, girl," one of them calls, "you walking backwards." Nod. Wave. Smile all the way to the cup of ice cream in the gutter. Pick it up. Take one bite, and then another. Don't stick your thumb out, exactly, so much as view the nail from a distance, arm stretched out. When a car whizzes past, enjoy the way your thumb remains steady as your heart pounds.

Know that next time you will be braver. You will not let anyone tell you what to do.

body language

ere is Lucha: on the last night of the Plant City Strawberry Festival, she's watching the Ferris wheel, the one thing she can see from the highway, blink lavender and gold over cars of outstretched hands. Once her dad has parked the Dodge, she can see more: whirling lights and lines of kids. Food stands and bulb-lit ticket booths. This is her first Strawberry Festival, the final hurrah before her family leaves Florida for the onions in Georgia, the tobacco in North Carolina, the pickle-cucumbers in Ohio. Until this year, she's been dropped off at a neighbor's house while her dad, her stepmother Suzie, and her two brothers wave from the windows and drive away. But this year she is ten, and exactly one hour ago she'd stomped the second-hand ballerina slippers Suzie insisted she try on, and told her father she was old *enough*. Now she stands, still in her pink slippers, before lighted signs for the Zipper and the Adrenaline Drop, the Steel Eel, the Hurricane. She's been practicing her English the whole way from the trailer park, whispering to the back of her father's seat while her brothers—dropped off at the gate—laughed. But in the parking lot, Lucha is speechless. She's picturing the moment when she will belt herself in and take off down the track, neck whipping backwards, hands flush to the sky.

Her father and Suzie unpeel themselves from the car. Suzie, Lucha knows, has only come for the food. She's been talking about it all week. Tomorrow the family will pile into the car, their mattresses strapped on top, and drive eight hours north to another field of ankle- or knee- or waist-high plants, and they'll spend another six months picking food for other people's dinner plates. But tonight, they'll eat. Here, strawberries come in as many ways as you can dress them: in cream, chocolate-dipped, on-a-stick. Cooked in butter, rolled in sugar. Frozen, freeze-dried, caramelized, canned. Lucha's brothers ignored Suzie, but while Lucha doesn't like her stepmother either, something about the way Suzie said "strawberry pie" made Lucha want to be nicer to her. Now Suzie and her father are joining hands, her father patting the bulge of wallet in his pocket like just for tonight, he's a rich man.

Suzie pats the corners of her mouth with a 7-Eleven napkin. Lucha inhales deeply the humid air. Beyond her, the enormity, the flexed muscle, the bend of the moving rides.

Music starts. Crowds balloon.

Lucha's father picks the Tilt o'Whirl for them to ride first, and Lucha forgives him for coming along when he lowers the bar into her lap, leans over, and says, "Éste es mi favorito." As the ride lurches forward, she laughs, fists clenched around the silver bar, kicking out one leg at a time. Her father is crushed against her one minute, sliding away in a lump the next. He howls when they spin past a line of people holding tickets, a white tent with a sign for Chinese Acrobats, Suzie nipping a fried turkey drumstick. The car creaks. Lucha removes one hand from the bar and holds it near the side of her face, not exactly in the air, but close. She touches the bar lightly with the other hand, then lifts it, too. Her father's hair blows back from his forehead. He glances down at her, raises his own hands from the bar. Together, they skate back and forth across the seat.

The bar rattles loosely, and then, after one gut-wrenching swivel, the pressure of eight festival nights causes a nail to bend, a clasp to slip free of its sleeve. The lock opens, and the safety bar swings free. There's a moment of sickening release before gravity pins Lucha and her father to the back of the seat. Lucha's father catches her shoulders. He braces his cowboy boots against the floor her feet don't yet reach and shouts for the attendant to stop the ride. The air is close in their faces, and the other cars fly maniacally around them. Lucha is breathless. She's the youngest in her family, and the only girl, so all her life people have fussed over her, belting and barring her in, catching her in child restraints and life preservers, keeping her back with lame excuses: "Sorry, Lucha, maybe when you're eleven." She's half-terrified, half-exhilarated. She wishes her father would let go. That the attendant would speed the ride up.

The Tilt o'Whirl unwinds, finally, but Lucha's eyes move in circles long after she's on solid ground. She steadies herself on Suzie's skirt fold while her father curses the ride attendant in English.

"Cheap American metal," he yells, flecks of spit hitting the boy's face.

"It ain't my fault," the boy says, towering over her father, red apron overflowing with used tickets, and he keeps saying this until her father turns his knotted brow, kicks the ground with a cowboy boot, and leaves.

"See?" he says to Lucha, as if this wins an argument they've not yet had. "See?"

Suzie looks down at Lucha, her upper lip thick with turkey drippings. Lucha doesn't like Suzie because she spends all the family's money, but Suzie has made it clear she doesn't care what Lucha thinks. Suzie buys curlers and soda, and department store underwear, and hair extensions, but when she tries to extend Lucha's hair, Lucha screams. So instead, Suzie tells Lucha to comb her hair, and cuff her jeans, and didn't she think it'd be easier to change her name to Lucy? Now Suzie holds out a thigh bone, picked clean. "Bite?" she says.

Ten minutes later, though her father is still talking about the Tilt o'Whirl, Lucha is all eyes for the Mamba. It's a wooden roller coaster—two loops and a screaming tunnel. A wind lifts out of the ground, buoys dust and wrappers and farm smells at Lucha's feet when she begs her father to let her ride. The purr of the Mamba is in her mouth. She uses English words, some of which her father won't understand.

"Pida Suzie si ella va con tu," he says, waving her away, but before Lucha can even balk, Suzie is eyeing the line and shaking her head.

"Not me," she tells Lucha, licking the nuts from a caramel apple. "I'm not waiting in all that."

The line stretches backwards clear to the popcorn stand, dotted with cowboy hats, farmhands, pockets of pierced kids not much older than Lucha sporting mohawks and cussing at each other, smoking and lighting bits of paper on fire. Lucha wishes her father and Suzie would go to the country music stand, leave Lucha to sashay up to the girl with hair in pink cones, eyes and boots rimmed silver, a chain running from her left ear to a ring through her eyebrow. Lucha would ask the girl if she could cut in line. She watches the girl talk, thinking that she would change her name to Lucy if only she could taste the girl's cigarette. She'd press her lips around the filter, the way women in the trailer park did, *nasty girls*, Suzie said, *and you better hope you don't turn out like that*. Lucha would force her tongue to pronounce the words without accent: *shit, damn, motherfucker, cowfucker, bitch*. Her jaw moves to the rhythm already, her tongue flat against the roof of her mouth. At school, girls like this made fun of her, mimicked her r's, her sibilant s's. Lucha scores better on vocabulary tests than they do, but she cannot force the words from her mouth the proper way. They call her *spic*, and her teacher corrects them. *Spanish*, she says, and though Lucha can pick Spain out on the map, she's never been there. Lucha likes the other word, the bad one, lips pursed like a kiss, then tongue hard against the back of her throat. This is what the ESL teacher in her last school taught her: feel where your tongue is. Put it in the right place. "Your language is based on rhythm," the teacher had said, tapping her heart. "English is all in the mouth."

Inside the Showcase Tent, where Lucha's father has dragged them, Grupo Vida belts out Tex-Mex melodies that are the consistency of soggy tortilla chips. Lucha's father claps along and tries to swing Suzie on his arm, but Suzie shoos him away with a fried cheese stick. She's studying the awards case, trophies for the baby race, the swine weigh-in, the Strawberry Queen. When Lucha tries to look, Suzie tells her not to bother.

"They don't even let girls like us on the Strawberry *Court*," Suzie says, "let alone the Queen. Once, a long time ago, they let a black girl in. She was a Duchess, I think."

Lucha knows Suzie is wrong. Her skin is dark, like her father's, but it's not called black here. Those are other girls, with their own sets of names. Suzie buys big jars of SPF 30 sunscreen she tries to get Lucha to rub on her arms. Her hair is bottled blonde and permed, swept back in a turquoise clip. She wears bright lime-colored scarves and hot pink blouses. Lucha's father says Suzie is his tropical bird. But Lucha has never seen Suzie like this: running a finger over the photograph, the crown, then lightly touching the top of her own head.

"It turned out she was illegal," Suzie says. "She got deported."

"Who cares about the court?" Lucha says by way of camaraderie, but Suzie's face stiffens.

"What do you know?" she says. Then, "Tie your slipper."

Suzie reaches toward Lucha's shoe, but she moves too fast, and without command, Lucha's fist shoots from her side, nailing Suzie right in the gut.

Suzie recoils, startled, her mouth open in pain. Lucha drops her hands automatically, like if they're at her sides no one can accuse her of doing anything, thinking anything. Suzie glares at her, and Lucha guesses that Suzie is thinking of the letters from teachers, the voices of other parents: *Lucha hits.* She hits fast and with severity, she hits before she has time to think, she hits like there's something in it for her. She hits because it is the one language in which she can make herself perfectly understood.

She hits, but she also bites, if she has time. It's the only thing she can rely on her mouth to do well. She counts her teeth by biting her own forearm. When she bites kids at school, her tongue moves up and back, the tip hanging suspended in the dead center of her mouth, the same way it does when she says "Hi" to the girls who call her *spic*. The same way it does when she whistles. She tries not to lick the kids she bites; she doesn't like the way they taste.

Lucha, she has heard teachers decide, is hard to manage.

That thought, and worse, is in Suzie's glare. Suzie glances behind her, at where Lucha's father is clapping, but Suzie knows better than to make a scene. If Lucha's father were to come over, he would laugh and say, "That Lucha is a feisty one." Then he'd take her outside, like he always takes her from school, and buy her something: a strawberry float. Lucha waits, almost interested in what Suzie will do next.

The waiting is a dare. Suzie accepts.

Suzie reaches out like she might pat Lucha's shoulder, if she were a patting kind of woman, grabs the skin where a breast might be, and pinches. This gesture, Lucha knows, has a name like a ride: a Titty Twister.

Lucha recoils, pain shooting through to her shoulder. "Bitch," she says. She cups her breast, and Suzie holds her stomach. They stare at each other.

Grupo Vida putters out, one maraca at a time, leaves a silence still as the gleaming trophies. In the bleachers, Lucha's father applauds. He stamps his feet, demands more, but the noise isn't loud enough to mask the emptiness of the Showcase Tent. Suzie wheels around to the trash can, drops her licked-clean stick into it, and wanders over to Lucha's dad.

"Lucha says she wants to go home," she says in Spanish, just loud enough for Lucha to hear.

"What about the fireworks?" her father says.

"She's too tired," Suzie says. She glances back at Lucha, who is watching with gritted teeth.

"I am not," Lucha shouts.

Suzie turns her back on Lucha. "Maybe we could take her to the kiddie rides," she says.

One of the Grupo members, a tall man with soap-colored skin, winks at Lucha as he exits the stage. He points at her feet, says, "Are you a dancer?" He is huge, leathery, horsey. His feet are pigeon-toed, his eyes yellow. When she doesn't answer, he repeats his question in Spanish.

Lucha clamps her teeth and stares hard. Then she uses another kind of language she is sure he'll understand. She raises her arm and extends her middle finger.

Across the tent, her father's gasp echoes. "Lucha," he hisses. "You see what I mean?" Suzie says, looking right in Lucha's eyes. "Lucha is a lost cause."

The exotic petting zoo is a poor replacement for the Mamba, but it's the one place her father will let her go alone. The wooden gate smacks behind her as she enters. Her father stands on the other side of the fence, cradling a llama muzzle in his hands. Lucha has a quarter's worth of food pellets in hers, too much to hold. She drops some with every step.

"Lucha," her father yells. "Use both hands."

But she's already letting more fall through her fingers, attracting a gray goat with white eyebrows. Her father beams. This is the kind of picture he loves, has pointed out to Lucha in commercials and picture books: a girl in a white dress, feeding sheep on a hillside. There is no white dress. There is no hillside. The animals in the petting zoo are llamas with matted fur, kangaroos with desperate eyes, a giraffe with parasites. But Lucha performs for her father, anyway, in the hopes of softening him up—she's still hoping for a chance at the Mamba. She feeds the goats a finger-scoop of brown pebbles, and they wander close to her, then away. Earlier, she'd watched as a kid tried to set a goat free, holding open the gate and offering it a chicken bone. Now the goat is on its knees, straining to reach someone's cup near the fence post. Hooves slice through piles of their own waste, scummy teeth strip splinters from the fence posts and chew. The smell is distinctly animal, distinctly caged. Miniature horses trot corner to corner nervously, stepping on chickens, laying out goats, their shorn manes twisting until the petting zoo attendant wrangles them into individual pens. "Must be the weather," he says, tipping a ball cap and curling his lip.

The goats are greedy; one almost takes her finger off. A line of blood appears on the crease of her pinkie. The giraffe won't respond to anyone, and several men—including Lucha's father—joke that it's died on its feet. While her father is yucking it up over the giraffe, a kid sneaks up behind Lucha and pokes her shoulder blade. Lucha reels, hackles rising on her neck, but the boy leaps out of hitting range and sticks out his jaw. He wears a festival T-shirt and a safari hat with a speckled feather in the band. The toes of his boots curl upward, as if they're brand new.

"What's the matter with you?" he says.

"Nothing."

"What happened to your finger?"

Lucha looks down at her blood-dripping finger, holds it higher for the boy to see. She says, "Your stupid goat."

"'Your stu-peed goat,'" the boy mimics, the words sliding over his teeth: he's making fun of her accent. He kicks the ground with his boot until he's made a hole, then bends over to wipe the dirt from the toe. "It's not mine," he says. "It's my uncle's." He points to an attendant draped over the wooden gate, talking to Lucha's father. The uncle smacks the giraffe on its haunches, and it jumps. The men laugh. Lucha hates them all, in this moment. Even her father. Especially her father.

The uncle smacks the giraffe again, and Lucha wills it to rear up, bare its yellow teeth, wrap its neck around the uncle's throat and squeeze. She wants the giraffe to find its legs, clear the fence, give the men what for. Instead, it looks like it might buckle. The legs hold, but shakily, and Lucha feels her cut begin to burn. She doesn't want to look at her father, so she watches the roller coaster instead. The Mamba is soaring, cars rattling on the wooden track. The boy follows her eyes.

"You ride that yet?" he says.

Lucha squeezes her finger so more blood oozes out.

"I got a friend who works there," the boy says. "He'd let you on, even if you're too short."

Lucha looks back at her father, his laughing face among all the other laughing faces. Suzie is drinking a soda, picking paint off the gate. Neither of them pays attention to her. They expect her to stay here, a good girl, with the babies and caged animals.

She follows the boy to the back of the petting zoo. She drops the feed in her hand, and it scatters like marbles. One by one, the goats come with their spare tire bellies, their flaking horns, their mouths parted to the ground. She does not look back. No one stops her.

Lucha latches the gate behind her.

The line for the Mamba goes underneath the roller coaster: rotting wood, bleakness, more hazy than dark. Yellow-green clots of light dangle from naked bulbs suspended by electrical cords from the scaffolding; their centers teem with mosquitoes. This reminds Lucha of the haunted house in a semi-truck that comes to the trailer park on Halloween. The air is congested. Lucha waits with the boy among throngs of kids, some of them French kissing, some smoking. Little boys run through the line, tripping and smacking their faces on the ground. The older kids laugh. They snake through the roped-off line, passing each other, watching each other.

"Hey," a blonde boy yells to Lucha. "¿Yo habla espaniol?"

He toys with a girl's collar; she grips his waistband. Lucha and her boy are silent. Above, the Mamba rushes by in a fury of sparks and noise. The track lists, trembles. Lucha memorizes the scene: the sound of her teeth grinding. The moonstruck dazzle above. The invisible breathing and blinking of the hot bodies around her—their stillness, their dead weight.

A breeze kicks up, and Lucha feels the grit on her neck. Then it is the boy, his breath behind her ear. She pushes him away, but in a minute he's back, holding her shoulders, pressing into them.

He smells like the goats. "Quit it," Lucha says. She pushes hard, but not as hard as she can—she doesn't want to be sent away for fighting. He steps backward, stumbles into a girl, a teenager, sitting on the rail in a section of line behind them. The girl turns, catches him around the neck. She looks at Lucha with ice blue eyes, rock-hard hair.

"He bothering you?" she says, and Lucha nods.

"You bothering her?" she asks the boy, and he shakes his head.

"I had the same problem with my stepdad," the girl says to her friends. "I called it sexual harassment. He called it parenting."

Her friends chuckle, and Lucha isn't sure if the laughter is directed at her, or the boy, or themselves. The girl blows Lucha a kiss before she jumps down from the rail and moves away with the line. Lucha circles by her several more times, and every time, the girl does something different: smiles crookedly, sticks out her tongue, makes an obscene gesture with her fingers and her mouth. Lucha isn't sure if she should smile, but she does anyway. The boy ignores her completely. His arms when they enter the darkest part of the line are white-blue, like detergent, the night foaming around them. Lucha's heels dig into the dust with each step, as if she's fighting for ground. As if the line, and the boy with it, might move on without her. She holds her spot, her square of Lucha-space, arms stretched so her hands reach the rails on either side of her. They laugh at her, the flashing, winking older kids, but they do not dare shove her aside.

The top of the steps yields the entrance to the ride. Here, even the apathetic, the cynical, entertain a jolt of excitement. The cars are shaped like rockets. Silver bodies, yellow tails, cherry red noses. Two across, four per car, ten cars to a train. Lucha watches kids vie for the front seat: a girl with black lipstick, a boy in a white bandanna. There is a jumble of words over the loudspeaker, an automated voice announcing rules and restrictions—*pregnant women should not* and *people with high blood pressure*—and an enormous digital timer counts down from ten.

The line thrusts forward, pulling Lucha through the turnstile that spills her onto the platform, and then she's in front of the ride. There's a moment of confusion where everyone gets to choose which car they want. The boy wins a spot in the front seat by elbowing a little kid, and he claims his prize triumphantly. They are separated, then. Lucha has been too slow, and must wait for the next round. She chooses an empty slot, four cars from the front. The boy in the front car surges forward without her, catapulting into the night beyond the doors. She wonders if he'll tell on her when he gets back.

When Lucha turns, the next train—her train—is nosing down the track. It is love at first sight.

An attendant comes by, telling everyone to step behind the red line, and he pauses over Lucha. He has a yardstick in one hand. Lucha looks away, hoping he'll move on.

"How tall are you?" he asks.

Before Lucha can think of an answer, there is disorder behind her. "Wait," someone is yelling, and for a moment Lucha thinks it's Suzie, come to take her away. "I'm with her," the voice says, and it is the girl with blue eyes shoving her way forward, catching Lucha's arm. "I'm her cousin."

Lucha tries not to grin. She gazes innocently at the boy and nods.

The dense night. The safety bar heavy in her lap. Lucha rigid in the seat, a girl's ponytail cutting the air in front of her, her pink slippers untied, the seat of her pants cold. The boy is somewhere on the ground by now, maybe back at the petting zoo, maybe winning a plush penguin by throwing darts, or rings, or basketballs.

But Lucha is flying. Jaw set, eyes wet with wind, she's allowing the girl next to her to unclasp her hands from the bar, straighten her elbows, reach upward with her whole body. She lifts out of her seat on the first loop, and but for the bar she'd be falling. She points her toes, spreads her fingers. The festival is a mishmash of light and ride—the teacups, the octopus, the swings—but she finds that if she concentrates she can see the detail around her, places where the chains are rusting away, the names carved into the seats.

At the top of the third hill, the coaster slams to a stop. The kids in front of her turn their windblown heads from side to side, crane over the edges of their cars, spit and catcall below. Lucha lowers her hands slowly. She glances at the girl beside her.

"What's your name?" the girl says.

Lucha is stiff-tongued and tight-lipped. "Lucy," she tries in her best accent. "I'm not Spanish."

"Me, neither." The girl grins, full-mouthed, revealing a row of glossy teeth. She reaches deep into her jeans and withdraws a pack of cigarettes. Marlboros, two r's, a difficult name. She shakes one out as the wind picks up, bends trees nearer to the rides. They sit for five minutes, then ten. Lucha asks the girl if it was true, what she said about her stepdad. The girl nods.

"I would've beat him up," Lucha says.

"Yeah?" the girl says.

"I punched my stepmom," Lucha says.

The girl props her arm on the side of the car and tilts her head to look at Lucha from one eye. "You're pretty tough," she says.

Lucha smiles.

"Was that your boyfriend back there?" the girl says, and Lucha stops smiling. She shakes her head. The girl inhales deeply. "Yeah," she says, "you didn't look very into him."

"I'm not," Lucha says. "I'm not into him."

"He was sure into you." She stretches her thin arms, leans over the side, and spits.

"He wanted to kiss me," Lucha says. Then she feels embarrassed, like a little kid. But the girl doesn't seem to notice. She sighs.

"Just wait. Pretty soon, that'll be the least of your problems."

Lucha must look confused, because when the girl glances over again, she does a double take. "Hold on," she says, slapping her hand on Lucha's leg. "Have you ever done that? Kissed someone?"

Lucha stares at the hand on her leg. Wishes the ride would start.

"It's easy," the girl says, situating herself as if for a long explanation. Then she leans in, tips Lucha's chin up with a single finger. "Start with your lips," she says, speaking into Lucha's mouth, "and then your tongue." Lucha feels the girl's tongue worming its way into her mouth, sending shock waves through Lucha's body. The kiss is fast, instructive, but when the girl leans back, Lucha feels winded. With the girl's mouth on hers, she'd felt adept, controlled. She wants it to happen again.

Instead, the girl peers over the side at the people gathering below them. Several minutes pass in silence. "So, Lucy," the girl finally says, "I'm sick of this. How about you?" Before Lucha can say yes, the girl throws off the safety bar. "Let's get out of here."

Lucha thinks she will follow this girl anywhere, but when she looks over the side, she feels dizzy. In the crowd, she spots her father and Suzie, peering up at the cars, trying to pick her out. Beyond them, in the distance, the slow movement of the petting zoo.

The boy, she knows, has ratted her out.

"Lucy? You coming?" the girl says, halfway onto the track.

"You can't climb down," Lucha says. "You're not allowed."

"Watch me," the girl says, and her face disappears below. Lucha leans over the car, watching the girl take the stairs two at a time, then flinging herself over the edge. She disappears into the festival. On the other side, Lucha notices her father pointing up at her, saying something to Suzie.

When the fireworks start, Lucha is still sitting suspended over the festival. She senses ears turning with the wind. Hairs rising. In the petting zoo, she can just make out the ponies, running like things possessed, like if they only went fast enough. If. A flock of birds rockets from a nearby banyan tree, like shattered pieces of the same animal.

The explosions of the fireworks are nearly enough to shake the cable cars from the sky, to tip the loops of the Mamba on its side. Lucha looks for the girl, can't find her. She removes her slippers, one by one. Tosses them over the edge and watches them spiral to the ground. Then, satisfied, she replaces the safety bar. She waits for the ride to start again.

When it does, Lucha's eyes are closed. She is kissing the air, first with her lips, then her tongue. She finds, suddenly, that it's easy to control her mouth. Just before the machinery catches and the ride shoots forward, she makes her lips do it again.

fortune

It's like this: when I was at the Rex parade during Mardi Gras and this man smelling like sucked crawfish heads came up and fed me a line about how he wanted to work my sweet all kind of ways, I had one foot about to slog it on out of there and one hand ready to sock him in the perversity. I'd been weaseling my way up to the front row so I could get a look at the Queen when she came floating by up top a decorated flatbed. I noticed him, this dude with three strings of gift shop beads around his neck, and I looked away when I saw him eyeing me. I knew he wasn't harmful—just some lawyer-banker-CEO-type cocksucker from the north who'd whisper stink at you in public but wasn't dangerous unless he got you alone in a gold-plated hotel on Royal Street, which he would call Rue Royale. Dangerous for some Kansas cowgirl drunk off her first yard of beer, but not me. I knew he wouldn't try nothing evil in public, and in front of a slew of one-use-camera tourists to boot. He might cop a feel, but I was ready for that. Hand positioned, like I say.

Then J., this guy who I didn't know well, who did street shows that always ended in arrest for petty theft, hustled up like somebody'd smacked him, spit stringing out the corner of his mouth pit-bull-style, and he whomped the guy so hard it looked like he flung his face three inches off his skull.

"What you did that for?" I yelled because I'm not afraid to holler at strangers. I was thinking, *Defended my honor, that's what*, but J. didn't say anything, and just as well because if I'd had any honor left, I think I would've sold it to one of those float drivers that'll let you ride in the cab for twenty bucks. What I wouldn't give for the chance to ride with those debutantes all done up in white like they made of soap bubbles. I'd even settle for the theme floats, Tabloid Headlines of the Bayou this year. I could be a Cajun Octuplet or Jerry Springer Guest or a Voodoo Doll.

J. says, "I don't know why I did it," and that makes me feel *terrific*, let me tell you. That's what I love about J., though, right from the start he didn't say nothing he didn't mean. I knew we had to get the hell out of there fast, and J. was looking dazed like he was the one been hit, so I pulled him by the forearm—kind of tugging and pulling my weight—and some guy in the crowd said, "Go, man, go," and that northern cocksucker squirmed around so he could see where we went, screaming about *Jesus Christ* and *Where's the fucking law*. We jumped the barricade in front of Tabloid Trash and lit out for the other side. I must've been in every back alley downtown, uptown, and across the river, so I found us a spot in a tunnel-dark corner where some rats were making fair game of loose trash.

"Why'd you do that?" I said again because I didn't know how to make nice introductions or nothing, even though I liked him, liked the looks he kept giving me, like he was trying to figure out why he was sharing time with a stick-skinny street girl and an army of rats. J. wasn't no looker by debutante standards, but he looked good to me, you know how they say, like the hero I never needed but wanted, maybe, now and then.

"I seen you by the ferry," he said. Then he told me we were like two ferries meeting for the first time on the river, and both of them alone until the other pulled up, and now I had a *poet* on my hands, and all I could think was, *Damn, I want to kiss this boy*. My lips were puffed up from sweating and my shirt stuck to my back where a bra would've been if I had any honor, but I felt better than the Queen I never got to see because J. didn't care nothing about the parade or all the tourists he could scam, he was sitting in the alley with me. And when a rat crawled too close, J. hit that, too, like the man, and it died on the spot, no blood or nothing. My psychic, Madame Vera, who says I'm almost too skinny to have a fortune, says, "Frankie, a good man don't draw no blood," and I thought she meant my last boyfriend—a face smacker—but now I knew she was talking about J. and the way my whole life could've turned out decent. My skinny old future was sitting across from me with a fury in his hands strong as moving water, and me the only thing that could stop it.

Can't say I ever cried much, but I cried then due to that rat still twitching in its tail and J. with those big hands that I wanted underneath my shirt. I scooted over (I got no grace, none at all) and kissed him, and he put his hands right where I wanted them, and things were all right. I didn't want nothing else, just J. and the street and the smell of piss and booze in the gutter. I was glad about that cocksucker, I wanted to chase him down and hug him because nobody's ever done for me like J. did, and when a man like that wakes up and sees you by the ferry it's a damn miracle. So there's me, nothing but skin and more skin Madame Vera says, crying over this con man named J., telling him, "My name's

Frankie," over and over. I could've swum the river right then, ferries or no.

The cops were tied up with Mardi Gras most of the night, so they didn't stumble into us until near morning. Me and J. had a whole day to dream up a life together, and I guess that's the way I always do it, use up my future in a single afternoon. They didn't catch me, the cops, even though they knew me by face, because I could squeeze through the places they wouldn't look. I left J. getting sober in his sleep, and I went back to the parade route where thousands of cocksuckers were dipping in and out of to-go daiquiri places and top- and bottom-less strip joints, and a few of them who didn't know they were waiting for me getting loose in the pockets. I'm no ferry boat, you know, and I've learned that listening to poetry will only get you through the night once, and even then you wake up hungry. The street was bright, like when you wake up and the light's so big it hurts and everybody's face is a scrambled TV screen, but I stayed there dancing to myself until the sweepers came out and cleared a lot of the trash away. I knew it didn't matter if I ran into J. tomorrow and he pretended not to see me, and if he called me a whore loud enough for me to hear, because he'd smacked that cocksucker for me, only me, and that was enough. I had him in my head forever now, harder than tattoo on muscle. And later, when I told Madame Vera about him, she said she could see the memory of J. in my palms, like a scar. Like I'd grown new skin. And isn't that just like a man, she said, to try to rewrite a fortune?

straitjacket

I. Pecos Pete

Friday night we score five hundred off a blind man. I hold him down, my friend Saint goes through his pockets. We're sitting out back the First Plus ATM on Belvedere, one of those ancient machines with plastic push buttons and a green screen wedged into the brick side of a bank that's been closed for months. This guy wanders up out of nowhere, white cane and everything. He thrashes around while I pin him but settles down once I've got my knee in his chest.

You're robbing me, aren't you? he says.

Saint is up to his wrist in the guy's pants pocket, but he looks up and says, Bingo.

Oh, man, the guy says. I'm getting robbed.

Then he starts laughing. Giggling, tears in his bleary eyes. I'm thinking I need to get some of whatever he's on—I'm so hard up tonight my teeth are chattering—but when I look through the bushes in front of the bank there are two cars stopped at a traffic light a few feet away. I slap the guy's face a couple times.

Quiet down, I say.

It's cool, the guy says. This is great. I've never been robbed before.

I can't believe this guy. I say, It's not supposed to be funny.

That's when Saint pokes me in the back with his elbow. I turn slowly, like I'm irritated, but lose my cool when I see the fat wad of cash he's holding.

Shit, I say. How much?

Saint peels off the bills—twenties. I'm going to cry, man, he says. I'm going to fucking cry.

And he does, the pansy. There I am, holding this mother-fucker down by the throat, and Saint's wiping his eyes with his gun hand. He licks his thumb so he can separate the bills.

How much you got there? I ask the blind guy.

Five hundred, he says. Take it. It's government money. I blow it on coke.

Government? I say.

State of Ohio, the guy says. They send it to me every month. Every damn month. I don't even want it.

Saint thumbs through the money, and the traffic light changes. Just take it, the guy yells. Take it. Take it.

I put my hand over his mouth until he looks like he's calmed down enough to talk normally. I'm nervous because we're so close to the street, but also because this seems too easy. I look in the windows across the street and in all the parked cars I can see, but there's nobody out besides me and Saint. I tell myself to keep a lid on the paranoia and chill out.

The fucking government, the guy says when I let him speak again. That's where the real crooks are.

Hear that? I say to Saint. We're not real crooks.

No, the guy says, it wasn't an insult. I like you guys. You're real. I'd rob me if I was you. Fuck big business. Fuck disability and Social Security. You have the most honest profession there is. Hell, you're my heroes.

That stops us. Nobody's ever said that to us before. And even though I know it's a line, the guy sounds so sincere that I can't see jamming my knee into his lungs anymore, especially since we've already got the money and he's not even trying to get it back. Saint steps away and I fall back, and we both stand to the side, watching him get up. He moves his head like he's trying to hear our breathing or something, like he can figure out where we are by the noises our bodies make, which is just the kind of freaky shit I've heard blind people can do.

Thanks, man, Saint says.

The guy's head snaps around to where Saint's standing. He bows. Thank you, he says.

We watch him walk off without the cane, feet feeling for the curb. When he's gone, Saint goes on and on about how, blind or not, the man saw us for who we really were. About how the guy could see.

Us, man, Saint says, thumping his chest. Me and you, Pete. He saw us.

We're a couple of heroes, I say.

I'm saying, Saint says.

Four-star criminals.

Wasting our talents. Wasting them, man.

And that's what I love about my buddy Saint: somebody tells him he's a hero and he believes it. In a few days, by virtue of sheer repetition, he'll make me believe he is a hero, and that maybe I am, too.

The five hundred is enough to keep my teeth still for a week and to buy Saint a used Hispano revolver from the VIP Pawn Shop, but the following Friday we're back at the ATM. It's drizzling and cold, and Saint's lips are blue. When we arrived, the first thing he did was punch out the R and the L on the sign, so it says, "Fist Pus," which sounds about right to me. Since then, Saint has wandered off to sulk, muttering how he hates this place, hates the bank and the job, the fucking Ohio weather. He's a tall Irish guy, six-six, but doesn't wear it well. I've known him five years, since my wife Ella left me because I was one-dimensional. She's got a kid now, by another guy, but I've got Saint, ha ha, if that's any kind of trade. Saint's a mechanic who also fixes things like stereos and old guns. I happened to come into several car stereos after Ella left, and Saint happened to know how to get rid of them. That was how we became acquainted.

It's pressing our luck to return to the scene, but we're hoping the blind guy will show up again with another wad. Saint keeps talking about how we're heroes, victimized by the system. He likes to talk about The System. Also, The Man. And now, because of the blind guy, The Government. He's just started ripping into his theory when a woman—a prime target—pulls up in a Plymouth. Saint gets quiet, then he lies on the ground and puts his face in the dirt.

I can't do it, he says. Look at her. She's wearing rollers. I can't rob a woman wearing fucking rollers.

I take the Hispano from him. I tell the woman to give me her fucking rollers. She hands them to me one at a time, unwinding them from her hair with a look like I've asked her to take off her underwear. The machine cuts her off at sixty bucks. I take all of it, and keep the curlers. Her hair is lumpy and sagging.

Saint's still on the ground when I come back. I throw the curlers at him.

Some hero you are, I say. Let's go.

On the walk back to my place, Saint and I pass three cop cars. We stick to the alleys. We keep our heads low.

Fucking ATM, Saint says. You know what kind of time you get for that? For sixty bucks?

I know as well as he does, but I don't say anything. Sometimes you have to let Saint run his mouth a while to get him to shut up.

Then he starts telling me about these amigos of his who held up twelve ice cream trucks in one day, just for the hell of it. They were all over the news, he says. Nobody—not the newscasters, not the cops, not the dumpy bastards driving the trucks—knew whether to lock them up or root for them. They were overnight celebrities.

You know what kind of time they got? he says. Community fucking service. That's it. Nobody cared how much they stole. That's what I call heroic.

The difference between us and them, I say, is a good idea.

Hell, Saint says, I've got plenty of good ideas. How's this: city buses. Every time I'm on one, I'm thinking, Here I sit with thirty-some captive wallets. Nobody to stop me.

The driver, I say. Don't forget him.

That's easy. Shoot out the radio. Then it's one big stick-up.

Saint grabs the bandanna I'm wearing and ties it around his mouth. He makes guns out of his fingers and holds them at his sides. He twirls one.

Howdy, pardner, he says. What's your name?

I've still got his Hispano, and when I point it at him, he stops twirling.

You want to rob a city bus? I say.

It's the modern-day stagecoach, man.

He kicks me with the toe of his boot.

Get it?

I lower the gun so it's pointing at his toe. I say, And I suppose you're a modern-day cowboy.

Sure, Saint says. I'm a cowboy. And you—you're Pecos Pete.

II. COTA Bus Driver #18

I sneak a quickie in Worthington. In the Crosswoods parking lot, between a Tex-Mex restaurant and a Bar & Eatery, where the COTA #2 route begins. Ralphie's standing in front of Champs, where he works. He saunters across the parking lot in an undershirt that doesn't fit, standard line-cook issue, smeared with pico de gallo and melted cheese. He doesn't change shirts anymore, just strips off the apron and slides out the front door. He used to splash on cologne that I would smell on my uniform the rest of the day. Now when he's next to me, the smell of fajita steam makes my mouth water. Just seeing him, the tips of my fingers begin to melt. That's what I told my sister Carlene. I said, He makes you feel like the smallest parts of you are melting. She said, He don't make me feel nothing, and I laughed because she knew what I meant. I meant, me. He makes me feel.

I'm not usually like this over a boy, and a white boy at that. I'm not kidding anyone. Shoot, I'm pushing thirty myself. My hair is graying at the temples, and the corners of my eyes are pulling downward like they might crawl off my face. I've lost the time I could be good for anyone like Ralphie. He should be balling some biology major in tight jeans, or several biology majors, or the whole department. But when he comes around, I go into a trance. I can't stop him, he can't stop him. He steps onto the bus, and we go to the long seat in back. It makes the day worth it.

I met Ralphie because he rode the bus from work to school, back when he was trying to become a business major so he could make a lot of money and get out of here, live in a place where it was always warm. Not to say I'm slinking up to every fine boy who puts his dollar ten in the hole. In fact, I don't think I even noticed Ralphie the first time. I was running late—I'm always running late—and everybody at the stop was mad. We get a lot of college students on the #2, done up in bright color no matter what the season, backless tank tops or hooded ski jackets. From far away, they look like neon signs, all red and yellow and blue against the concrete. My uniform is gray, darker gray at the collar and cuffs. Ralphie says that doesn't matter because I have skin the color of love, and what do I need with a lot of fancy clothes?

The color of love. This is the kind of thing I never used to fall for.

When I'm running late, I try to ignore the students because they're always mad and wilting, and this day they were trying to give me foul looks, too. They don't dare say anything to me. They know I'll turn them off. Anyway, I figured Ralphie was another good-looking boy pissed off because he was going to be late to Theoretical Mathematics or something, some Lambda Lambda freshman commuting from Worthington. No, that's not true. I didn't figure anything then. Not until later. But that was how we met. He climbed aboard.

He sat behind me once, a couple times, then regularly. I get to know the regulars by face. Some drivers won't speak to anyone because of the crazies, but I kind of enjoy the crazies. They keep my mind off the road. Ralphie talked. I found out he wasn't any frat boy, and then I thought maybe he was a rich kid, taking the bus because of a DUI—we get a lot of those, too—but that wasn't true, either. He was friendly, the kind of kid used to making everyone around him like him. He was just nice. Imagine that. I got to talking myself, and before he got off I'd take an unauthorized break to keep talking some more, then have to haul it to the next stop. He was always waiting at the Worthington stop, and if I came a little early, he'd be waiting then, too. One thing, as they say. Led to another. Another meeting place, another ten minutes, another body part exposed. Now we're something of a habit, and every time I'm on the Number Two **#2?** he finds me, and then I have to rush to get through the next four stops. Sometimes I skip a couple. I drive by a crowd of students, their faces turned in disbelief to follow me down High Street.

I'm going to get fired for this. I've been warned. Twice. I know it, but I can't stop. It's been so long, if you know what I mean.

Carlene knows. She worries that Ralphie's demented, or a sicko. It's not right, she says, what does he want with you? I say he's no more sicko than me. It takes two, as they say, and we laugh at the coincidence. Two. The Two. We start calling the line Two to Tango. We have to talk in code. George, my husband, would not appreciate the joke.

George Jean, which makes me Mrs. Jean, but Ralphie never calls me that. Even though he knows. He calls me Honeybells. Hey, Honeybells, he says when he gets on the bus. This is a sweet ride you got here. I give him a sweet ride, all right. Carlene says I shouldn't talk like that.

When he leaves, it's back to the kitchen to dice tomatoes and shred cheese and squirt sour cream onto nacho platters, because he doesn't go to school anymore. He doesn't need it, he says, and I tell him I never went to college and I've turned out fine. But he's not happy about it, you can tell. I'll see you, Honeybells, he says when he leaves. I get the feeling he means he's thinking about me when I'm not there. If I know when I'll be back on the Two, I tell him. If not, he says he'll find me. He always does. Maybe it's just luck, and the luck will dry up someday. I'll get fired. I'll leave George, sign on as a waitress at Champs. Read messages into the salsa, like tea leaves. Like palms. I can feel the warm, white dishes in my hands. I can see his face fogging up the glass.

Anybody can chop vegetables, Carlene says.

I correct her. Dice, I say.

I try to explain. I tell her about winter on the bus. Snow sticks to the windshield. The air is the color of the road. The bus lurches and slides, and there are times when a gust of smog will blow in through the open door, and I feel the city itself climb aboard, move through the seats with steely limbs, gaze out the grimy windows with eyes of slate. I try to drive faster, to catch up, but at times like these, the instruments I have to work with—steering wheel, floor pedals, mirrors—seem about as useful as a sunroof in a rainstorm.

In the winter, even the crazies don't seem as crazy. They're just cold. When the body is cold, the body will do what it takes to warm itself. Craziness, like love, becomes a luxury.

This is what I tell Carlene. She understands I'm talking in code. It doesn't matter that it's not all true, that, in reality, the guy who mumbles and rocks in his seat in July is still rocking in January. That the pervert still has his dick in his hand in December.

III. The Peeled Eye

When asked, I tell women that the fundamental principle on which the Peeled Eye Exhibit rests is point of view. Then I define it for them.

Point, I say. To gesture towards. Also a summit, or, in writing, a thesis. View. To see, usually clearly, but also the object of such gaze. So then, we have point of view: to gesture toward a landscape. Or to call attention to the object of a gaze. Or my favorite: to see sight.

Here's where I normally pause for effect. Tonight I'm drinking Killian's, so I take a sip. The girl, who has told me her name is Heather, I think, is onto me.

Okay, she says. I'll bite. What's in the exhibit?

My finest work, I say.

The first thing you see as you enter is a camera filming you from a four-foot tripod cemented to the floor. Past it, a room of windows, residential next to high rise, cellar panes, portholes, stained glass. Beyond the windows, there are more cameras. And inside the room, the only exhibit is a straitjacket. Disembodied.

Here I lean back, give Heather time to puzzle through what I've said.

Sounds weird, she says, wrinkling her tiny nose.

It's strange how even after three weeks of hearing this response, it still causes my stomach to tighten.

The whole thing is very postmodern, I say. After viewing it, one woman actually ran from the room.

I can see that I'm losing her. She's bored silly by the conversation, but I can't help myself. I've been spending more time in my exhibit than, I think, is good for my mental health. I've become an empty room of windows myself. When I'm not talking about the Peeled Eye, I don't know what to say.

The challenge, I say, is how to force viewers to see their own gaze. See? This was my task. How well I fulfilled it, of course, is up for interpretation. You've read the *Dispatch* article?

I don't read papers, she says.

I believe this about her. She is tough, this girl, but not bright. She's beautiful, but that goes without saying. I would like to film her. I would like to film, then fuck her. Or the reverse. She reminds me of the graduate students who run the basement gallery where the Peeled Eye is installed, the Art History majors with long bangs and feminist interpretations of Cubism who keep calling to tell me they've decided to take the Peeled Eye down early and want me to collect the pieces. Mine was the second room in a series of five, and now they want to expand the one next door, an exhibit called "La Vie Est Lente," after Apollinaire. I tell people it means "Life is Boring," which isn't an exact translation. "La Vie" is composed of twelve torsos with nation-shaped bruises. There's the U.S., of course, and France. Some African countries, a few European ones, Australia, and Russia, which takes up an entire midriff and lower back. "La Vie" has popular appeal, and was the only reason the newspapers deigned to visit the gallery at all.

The *Columbus Dispatch*, I say, called my exhibit "voyeuristic and manipulative."

And what do you call it? the girl says.

Art, I say. And truth.

You're a pompous old fogey, the girl says, smiling.

She leans over and licks the cigarette out of my mouth. I think I have won her over again, but then, with my cigarette dangling from her lips, she says, Maybe I'll come see it sometime. And she leaves.

Sweetheart, I call after her. Then, sounding more desperate, Hey, Heather. She walks past the bar and out into the warm night. I contemplate following her, putting her hand in my groin and my tongue in her mouth. But this is not the part of town for that. I'm too close to campus, with its lighted walkways and call centers.

Of "La Vie Est Lente," the *Columbus Dispatch* said, "A sobering look at contemporary world politics, and the highlight of the show."

The last time I got laid was three weeks ago with an Art major whose hands shook as she unzipped me under the table. She worried me. *If you blab*, I'd warned her. I was all vim and vigor that night, but now, after Heather has gone, I feel deflated. Ever since the gallery started leaving messages on my machine, I've lost focus. Drive. I'm not sure where to go or how to get there. I leave the bar and drive to an upscale place on Fifth Avenue that has an indoor fountain with several goldfish. Bodies are packed close enough to create a smell, but no one notices me except the fish, which nibble my fingers when I dangle them in the water. The exhibit haunts me. I miss it. I have a shelf of tape for each of the two weeks it's been open to the public, and it's only when I watch them that I feel calm. Without the Peeled Eye, the world seems off-kilter, the pitch too flat and the focus slightly off. I've taken medicine, but I can't pinpoint the problem.

I fear that I have become my exhibit. You see why I can't let them take it down.

In twenty minutes I've spoken to no one, though I've watched a boy down a live goldfish, a meaty yellow one, on a dare. Someone snaps a picture, and in the flash, I imagine I see the tail pulsing his throat in and out as he swallows. Sickened, I decide to leave. As I push through the crowd to the door, a girl takes my hand. She breathes in my face, promises on her lips.

There you are, she says.

I say nothing. Her hand is warm, loose. She squints through her glasses, wrinkles a pierced nose.

Wait, she says. Oh, god. Sorry. Wrong guy.

I cling to her. I tell her I'm not the wrong guy, and that, should she come home with me, I'd make it worth her while. The words ring false. I have lost my touch, my sensibility.

She turns my hand over, pats the skin below my wrist.

How much? she says.

When I don't say anything still, she unwinds my fingers and releases herself.

Sorry, she says. I'm sure you're nice and all.

I drive to my apartment, where a new message is on my machine. Instead of listening to it, I take a stack of surveillance tapes heaped on a metal bookcase by the door to view. For three hours I contemplate the exhibit—how it's symbolic of our collective consciousness, the emptiness of our vision—until I nauseate myself. I stumble out of the room, into a hallway lit only by a red Exit sign, sink to the floor, and yell, loud as I can. The sound echoes through the hall, bouncing off the doors.

That's when it hits me. All I need is a better idea. Something bolder than "La Vie"—more daring, more artistic. Something the *Columbus Dispatch* won't be able to ignore.

What I need is the ugliness of real life: a girl who might or might not be named Heather walking out of a bar; a goldfish as it slides down a boy's throat. I imagine more cameras in the Peeled Eye, more videotapes. On one screen, a licked cigarette. On another, a flashbulb bursting.

Of course it's voyeuristic. Of course it's manipulative. But I know that the Peeled Eye isn't dead.

Not yet.

IV. The Heist

In Worthington, #18's back rubbed against the plastic cover on the long seat in the rear. Her shirt had pulled up, and the friction was giving her a strawberry on her left shoulder blade. On the bus ceiling, she thought she saw the face of the president (Clinton, at the time, though it could've been any president, anyone in a position of authority), and when she turned her head to moan, she saw someone peeking in the front window of the bus.

"Jesus," she said, pushing Ralphie up by his shoulders and swinging her legs to the floor.

"What?" Ralphie said. His voice cracked, the way it did when he'd been interrupted. #18 knew this. She'd made him stop before.

#18 put a finger to her lips, crouched, and tiger-crept to the front of the bus. She had no thought of how she must look to Ralphie. She didn't know what she'd do if she caught the peeper. She wasn't trying to plan, just act. When she raised her head to the level of the glass and peered out, no one was there.

The Peeled Eye had sensed danger and fled. He retreated to his bus stop to wait for the driver to finish. Normally he watched until she made oo oo sounds and clutched the white boy to her chest. He didn't get off on it. He liked that he knew something secret about his bus driver. It was sweet, in its way. He never ogled skin because they didn't take their clothes off. When the driver's nipple made an appearance, it was quickly covered by the white boy's mouth. Later, when the Peeled Eye climbed into the bus and scanned his pass, he'd try to give the driver a knowing look, but she would be focusing on the road, on windshield wipers or the right-hand lever that opened and closed all the doors. He'd sit in the back and try to feel her sex, what it had been like, an hour or so ago, to fuck a white boy.

"What's wrong?" Ralphie said, not like he really wanted to know but like he was inclined to ask, at times such as these—his woman tiger-creeping around the bus while his dick dripped down his work jeans.

"Nothing, honey," #18 said. She straightened her spine as if for confrontation. "I'm just antsy." It was Friday. On Monday, her boss had given her until the end of the week. There had been too many complaints, he'd said. But now #18 knew the truth. She'd been found out. She'd been watched.

"You want to go inside?" Ralphie said. He suggested a change of venue for most of life's and #18's problems.

"No," #18 said. She didn't want to go anywhere. She felt suddenly public.

"Come on, Honeybells," Ralphie said, hand in his crotch. "We don't have much longer." #18 could let herself melt into him, finger by finger, until he shielded her from the world. She could make him promise to meet her somewhere—a hotel room, an apartment. But that would mean that later, when George asked her if they had any milk, she might say, "No, George, we've never had any milk," and burst into tears. Everything felt like a confession these days. She wasn't even speaking to Carlene anymore because Carlene had said that if #18 didn't tell George, she would. Carlene liked George, she said, and was sick of being in the middle. Carlene didn't know what she was talking about. #18 was the one in the middle.

She never wanted to tell George what happened today with the peeper, not even if she told him everything else. She didn't want him to know how the world had looked in and seen how foolish she could be. #18 felt numbers start in her chest: sixteen screws in the back of the bus, fourteen orgasms, eight blow jobs for her, five for him, four times she'd broken into tears in the middle, twice laughter, twice he'd pinched her on accident, and once—once she'd found someone watching them. When she added them up, their sum was zero. Ralphie was just a boy who didn't wear cologne for her anymore. Body heat was not love. When her job ended, so would her affair. She was a married woman, with skin the color of road dust.

Ralphie zipped up and kissed her on the lips. She stood at the head of the bus, staring blankly. Ralphie didn't want a fight. He opened the door for himself, a bitter way to exit and not at all sweet.

"See you later, Honeybells," he said and believed that he would. He smoked a cigarette and walked back to Champs, thinking of #18, her long, drooping breasts, her watery eyes.

A pair of tomatoes like breasts on the counter, #18 thought, watching him walk away. Who had written that, way back when she'd been learning lines in high school? *And you with a twelve-inch serrated knife.*

The young women at the bus stops were dressed in scarves so colorful they were almost obscene. They were irritated and rushing because the bus was late—so late that #18 could see the head of the next bus inching into her side mirror. Pretty soon it would overtake her.

The Peeled Eye also noticed the scarves, but only after he'd scanned the faces perched atop them. They were irritated, yes—they might call it vexed—but in a way that suggested they'd forget their frustration in an instant given the appropriate distraction.

The Peeled Eye's problems, on the other hand, were more severe. Last night he'd been involved in a minor incident—it hadn't been his fault at all, really—but he supposed some people would call it a crime. People who didn't understand, who thought in terms of absolute morality when, in fact, there was so much gray. Another dimension of the Peeled Eye Exhibit was its infinite varieties of gray.

They'd taken it down, the bastards. Left the parts for scrap. And the Peeled Eye had been so upset to find his windows stacked in a closet, his camera dusty, that he'd gone a little crazy. He couldn't seem to let go of the camera. He'd taken it with him to the bar, where things had gotten even more absurd.

He'd drugged a girl. He'd drugged several girls, actually, but only the one had gotten in the car with him. He didn't even know what the drug had been—the guy at the bar who'd offered half his share to the Peeled Eye had called it Spanish Fly. Eight doses in lemon drops for a table of girls, then eight girls with swollen pupils trying to help each other out of their seats. The Peeled Eye had limited himself to one, a girl with horn-rimmed glasses who dry-heaved into his shirt after the deed was done. It'd been a rotten experience altogether, even after she'd passed out. Only a matter of hours ago, he'd been propping her body against a blue security post on campus and calling the police.

"I've found a girl," he said. "She doesn't have a shirt on."

As an afterthought, he filmed twenty seconds of her. He was a little drunk himself, and he laughed as he filmed, listening to the purring machinery next to his ear. This would be his new exhibit, he thought. The Peeled Eye, Phase Two.

"You'll be famous," he told her as he left. He'd walked halfway home, too nervous to return to his car, when he remembered that he'd left his credit card at the bar.

It might not be a problem. The card might be filed away in a lost and found box, or, better yet, thrown away. It was the might that made him dress down, sneakers and a T-shirt, for the bus ride to campus. He brought the camera, but tried to keep it inconspicuous. The tape with the girl on it was still inside. He wanted to blend in.

The Peeled Eye got off at Hudson, walked to High to transfer to the #2. Several other people made the same journey. The Peeled Eye was thinking, This is the final leveling ground. Like homeless shelters and unemployment lines and prison cells. On the bus, he wasn't an artist or a rapist. He was nobody.

The inside of a bus is a giant metaphor, the Peeled Eye thought. He almost laughed at the brilliance of it, of himself. Here we are, in no man's land. Purgatory.

It was as if he'd pulled Pecos Pete out of his brain. When they met at last, the Peeled Eye had trouble separating Pecos from his exhibit.

But Pecos was real—at least, he was a real man who'd dreamed up a formula to turn himself into a legend. He and Saint had spent all night in Pecos's apartment, where mold grew on the walls in stalagmite formations, so strong you could smell it at the front door. The mold was a new addition, and Pecos told Saint he expected for it to start paying rent any day now.

"Hope you're not allergic," Pecos said.

"Don't you know me by now?" Saint said, scraping mold off with his fingernail, and wiping it on his pants. "I don't get sick. I haven't been sick in twenty-five years."

"Fucking god complex," Pecos said. "I forgot." He got a beer for himself and didn't offer Saint one. He liked Saint, trusted him, but sometimes the guy could be a real prick.

They spent the night planning. They'd spent months planning, but they spent the night making the final touches, perfecting details, going over the route they'd take, and the backup route, and the backup to that. Everything had to be timed right. They'd tag five buses—enter, shoot out the radio, cock a gun at the driver's head—provided the cops didn't catch up. They repeated directions aloud, memorized lines. They'd focus on the college area and avoid their own neighborhood. On buses in their own neighborhood, people carried weapons. They weren't worried about dying. They were worried about things like exploded small intestines and ruptured stomachs and splintered shoulder blades. They already walked as if they had bullets lodged in their spines. Stiff. Straight. They'd been around and had come back for more.

And then, just before they left the house, Saint called three news stations.

"You're going to narc on us?" Pecos said. "Just like that?"

"Trust me," Saint said. "We're too good to get caught." He tied a bandanna around his face and looked into a dirty mirror on the wall. "Too good-looking," he said.

When he picked up the phone, Pecos didn't protest. The media wouldn't necessarily call the cops, he figured, especially if they were interested in the story. He imagined a glimpse of himself on a tape that the newscasters would highlight later, a hazy circled face, a composite sketched with too-big ears or the wrong texture of hair. He liked the idea of being both famous and anonymous. He liked that people would wonder who he was.

"High Street," Saint told whoever answered the phone. "Tell your people that they're going to get some serious live footage."

At the first stop, no one paid them any attention, even with the bandannas. The plan was to ride north, midway to downtown, and then begin. The first bus was a trial run—was, as Saint put it, a test of the gods' moods. When they entered the second bus, equipped with two guns, two backpacks, and two bandannas tied securely behind their heads, it was into the middle of a fight. A woman Pecos knew only as Dimple had been trying to breast-feed her six-week-old baby girl in a seat four up from the back. She was discreet, but not enough for Sharmane Grover, who told Dimple to "put it back in the holster, hon, nobody wants to see that." Dimple flipped her the bird and, from Pecos's perspective, pulled the baby back to expose even more of said nipple. Sharmane stood to a full height of five feet nine inches, puffed two discreet B-cup breasts up beneath her gold shirt, and demanded that Dimple leave the bus. She wagged her long fingers in Dimple's face, and looked to Pecos as if she might strike the woman, baby or no. The driver glanced into the rear view. Saint strode down the aisle.

"Sit down, ma'am," he said. He gripped Sharmane's shoulder, and people turned in their seats to watch. "Sit down."

Sharmane smacked his hand away, and Saint pulled his gun on her. Dimple started to thank him, then fell silent. Saint demanded her wallet.

"Shit," Pecos said. He'd been following Saint down the aisle, but now he hurried up front. He shot out the radio system with a rusty Texas Ranger, courtesy of the VIP, and someone screamed. He forgot his lines. The bus driver started to pull over, but Pecos jerked the steering wheel.

"Keep going," he said, breath hot under the cloth.

In the back, Saint shouted instructions. The baby began to wail, and Sharmane, even though she was scared, managed to shoot Dimple a mean look. One man tried to pry open the rear door, but Saint threw him on the floor and stepped into his spine. Someone else, nobody knew who, pushed the Stop Requested strip. That made Pecos laugh. Stop requested. He gained composure, held the gun lightly at the driver's ribcage, out of view of the front window.

"Don't stop for that," he said.

In the end, the ride went smoothly. Smooth as sobriety, the Peeled Eye might have said, had he been there. The bus was only a quarter full, but Saint got fifteen wallets and six cell phones, which was more than they'd made in a week holding up ATMs. Pecos told the driver not to stop, not even to glance back, until he hit Broad Street downtown. He threatened a lot of stuff, including a bomb.

When they got off at King Avenue, Pecos looked up and down the street for the Channel Four news van, maybe Holly Hollingsworth, the anchor, sitting in the passenger seat. But there was no one, not even a stray cop to bust them for jaywalking.

"Shut up," he told Saint, who was whooping Hell, yeahs, and they crossed the street to wait for another bus to take them in the opposite direction.

That was the bus the Peeled Eye had caught twenty minutes ago. He'd gotten on and just kept riding. He didn't want to go home; didn't want to return to the bar. The bus seemed as good a place as any to film the new exhibit. When Saint and Pecos boarded, loaded down with wallets and cell phones and even a few laptops from the last two hits, the Peeled Eye was filming a fat woman picking cans out of the garbage. He had two hours' worth of tape, priceless tape he could never duplicate. The girl had been good luck: after her, genius had fallen right into his lap.

When Saint demolished the radio, the Peeled Eye jumped, swiveled, and got a head-on shot of Pecos storming down the aisle.

"You," Pecos said. "Give me your wallet."

The Peeled Eye lowered his camera without turning it off. When he realized what was happening, he was elated. What could be better, more trivial and yet more brilliant, than this—a mugging to end his collage? It made so much sense. Thievery, violence. A reversal of fortune. Morality turned on its head. The Peeled Eye smiled and held out the whole burnished leather ensemble. It was too perfect.

Pecos perked up when he saw the amount of cash inside. "You don't know this, man," he said, "but you're making our day."

The Peeled Eye looked up at Pecos. Neither man, they felt, belonged on that bus. They looked surprisingly similar: jeans, plaid shirts, sneakers. How they spent the ends of their days, that was where the difference was.

"I do know it," the Peeled Eye said. He imagined what he'd tell the cops. My license was stolen, he'd say. I can describe the man who took it.

Pecos hustled down the aisle to show Saint the dough—as much as the blind guy had given them, maybe more—but when he got there, Saint told him to put the money away.

"Fuck that," Saint said. "Dude's got a video camera."

He left Pecos up front clutching the cash, strutted down the aisle, and brought a gun to the Peeled Eye's temple. "We'll be needing this, too," he said, reaching for the Peeled Eye's camera.

The Peeled Eye was stunned. "You've already got my wallet," he protested. He held onto the strap and tried to kick Saint away.

Saint smacked him with the gun and took the camera. "This thing on?" he said.

"Give it back to me." The Peeled Eye felt his cheek begin to swell. "At least give me the tape. It's research. I need it."

"Research this," Saint said and smacked him again with the gun. The corner of the Peeled Eye's mouth began to bleed.

Pecos flinched when he saw the second blow. "Take it easy," he yelled.

"Fuck off," Saint yelled back, and he raised his hand again.

Somewhere in his flickering consciousness, the Peeled Eye regarded the beating with an artist's interest. This kind of intense physical pain was new to him. He wanted to remember it later. He counted the blows, and they stopped at five. The bus stopped, too. There was noise, commotion, then a loud banging at the Peeled Eye's window. He opened one eye and saw the man who'd hit him grinning on the sidewalk outside, camera on his shoulder. Filming him. The Peeled Eye hurt in more ways than he'd ever experienced before, but he managed to grasp and pull himself to the front of the bus as it began moving forward.

"Stop," he said from the part of his mouth that was still working. "Let me off."

The bus driver was crying. "Sit down," he said. "No one can leave yet."

The Peeled Eye clutched a metal bar in front of him. He was no longer amused, no longer an impartial bystander. He wanted to get to a pay phone. Even he—a man who believed in only the universal law of fate—had rights.

"We're going to Broad Street," the driver yelled for the whole bus to hear. "I can't stop any sooner."

The Peeled Eye fell onto the seat behind him. He watched buildings pass, a Mobile Gas Station, Suds and Spuds Laundromat, the Indian Kitchen, and then the university, the museum rising behind several flowering pear trees. Students lined the sidewalks, threw Frisbees on the lawn.

His face hurt. His head throbbed. He felt his exhibit heave and die. He gripped the seat and stared out the bus window like a convict.

Three blocks back, Pecos watched the bus's tail lights, and Saint smacked the camera with his fist. It was malfunctioning; it'd run out of tape.

"Fuck me," Saint said, and pressed rewind. There was a little TV where he could watch the tape in reverse: ten full minutes of a homeless guy sleeping on a bench. He and Pecos were waiting for the next bus. They were giddy but controlled. The plan had turned out to be smarter than they'd realized. The cops weren't stopping buses because to do so might cause panic, and they wanted to catch the thieves in the act. They'd had no doubt that they'd be able to spot the perps, until they started looking at bus stops. Then, it seemed, everyone looked like a criminal. Pecos and Saint watched two cruisers pass without incident.

"We're invisible," Pecos said. He was angry at Saint for what had happened on the last bus, and he knew things could still go wrong. But dammit, if they weren't almost done. If they hadn't almost done it.

"Where the hell is the news?" Saint said as the last bus pulled up.

#18 was right on schedule. When they boarded—Saint, then Pecos, minus the bandannas which they'd removed because of communication problems—she didn't look in their direction. She was staring straight out, flushed with uncertainty, as if she'd suddenly realized she didn't know how to drive and wasn't sure how she was going to break it to the passengers. The motor sputtered, the windows rattled. The bus was half-full.

Pecos put his hand on #18's shoulder. He noticed her fly was open. "Drive," he said. In the back, Saint pulled out his gun. A girl screamed. Two people covered their heads. The best part, Pecos thought, was how everybody acted exactly the way they were supposed to. He poked his own gun into #18's temple.

"Get that gun out of my face," she said.

"What?" Pecos said.

She turned, and the gun moved to the middle of her forehead. "I don't care what kind of dumb-ass prank you're pulling, if you want me to keep driving, you'll point that gun somewhere else."

Some of the riders looked at them, and Pecos was embarrassed. This was the kind of woman who'd bossed him around his whole life, just like his ex-wife Ella. He wasn't sure how to fight back except to hold his ground. "Just keep driving," he said.

#18 was thinking that she'd had about enough of everyone's shit. She'd passed a bus stop full of people—young professionals and truant high school kids and bored senior citizens—who looked at her with recognition, accusations on their lips. *Call*, she dared them. *Call and complain about me today.* She shoved the butt of her hand into the horn, which blasted and made the people on the sidewalk jump. She held it. She sped up. "Get the gun out of my face," she said again, with conviction.

Saint looked at Pecos in alarm. Pecos said, "Okay, okay," and moved the gun to the driver's ribcage.

When he'd finished with the wallets, Saint held up the camera and filmed the bus. "Yo, Pecos," he said, and Pecos gave him his worst scowl. He wasn't sure what Saint was going to do with the tape—send it to the news, probably—but he liked the feeling that looking into the lens gave him. "This is Pecos Pete," he said solemnly. Then he grinned. "Modern-day outlaw."

"Yee haw," Saint screamed, and he stood on a seat to get a good shot of the passengers. He zoomed into the face of a girl who was crying, an old man who looked like he had peed his pants. He got the back of the bus driver's head, then her face in the mirror. He turned the camera around and filmed himself, the trees rushing past the window behind him, his eyes fluorescent.

#18 counted police cars as she passed them. Three, then four. One of them would rescue her eventually, return her to George and her guilty conscience. Five. #18 wished there was another way. She imagined leaping from the bus doors at thirty miles per hour. Or hurling herself at the gunman, wrestling him to the floor, then springing back up to steer the bus to safety. It wouldn't take much to knock the weapon from his hand—one swift motion, and she'd be the one in charge. And what then? Shoot him? Grab the loot and make a run for it? Save the bus, demand her job back, return to Ralphie like nothing had happened? She pictured Ralphie where she'd left him, at Champs, food steam rising around his face, oil popping and onions sautéing, servers streaming in and out while he stayed calm in the middle, doling out meals for hungry, bored people. Sustenance for the rich and the dull, the ugly and the unloved. Ralphie fed them all, and fed them and fed them, and they left so full they could hardly breathe.

It was the camera that irritated her the most. It reminded her of the peeper, and of how long she'd been trying to hold on

to things: her job, her husband, her sanity. Ralphie. #18 felt suddenly cold. There was only one thing left to let go of. She kept
her foot on the gas and leaned back. No one was watching her.
The man next to her was grinning into the camera, the gun light
in his hand.

"George," she said quietly. "Oh, Ralphie."

For a minute, the bus sailed along like it was on rails. Then
the wheels turned slightly toward the curb. An adjustment, a
change in her route. A drift that #18 could still correct if she
wanted to.

vertical mile

❧

He was not the kind of guy you normally saw on the Bright Angel Trail. For one thing, he was fat—obese, if you wanted to get technical, though he seldom did—and presently he was shedding several pounds through sweat alone. For another, he wasn't dressed for hiking, certainly not for this kind of hiking, straight down into the hot pit of the canyon in jean shorts, a collared shirt, and sandals. The sandals fit snugly around his ankles and made his bare legs look twice as large as they did in knee socks, but he hated knee socks because they made him itch. He had no backpack or camelback, no supply of food or first aid. He carried a single liter of water in a sports bottle he'd filled from a fountain at the rim, and to him even that seemed more burden than it was worth. He, Marcus McConnel, had not come to the Grand Canyon to hike; he'd come to die.

If the hike didn't kill him, didn't wring out his overstressed heart and leave it dry, limp, then he planned to swan dive off a cliff. Still, he hoped not to get to that stage: the pain was what concerned him, that initial blow to the face on a craggy redstone outcropping—and then, if the first one didn't do it, as it was entirely plausible that it wouldn't, the second and, god forbid, the third—and the kind of pain people like him spent entire lives trying to avoid. He was counting on his heart, or one of those sorry excuses for organs crushed inside his chest, to give out long before he arrived at the bottom, eight miles below the surface, that spot he'd seen on the Chamber of Commerce brochure where the trail reached out like a bony finger to the tip of Bright Angel Point and ended in a guard rail, the canyon issuing forth in a stream of gold and bronze, clouds framing the horizon, a thunderstorm inching in from the west. Worlds away from the lunching tour groups he'd passed at the rim, the families and photographers and nature enthusiasts, the couples, the kids with sticky faces running too close to the edge. They'd watched his first lumbering steps in silence, marveling at his decision to embark on this most strenuous of trails, sandals biting into the dust as his weight poured downward, gravity sweeping over him like a black cloud.

Now, not ten feet from the start, a ranger with mirrored glasses was stopping him, suggesting, no offense, that he try a more level trail, or maybe he'd like a bus tour of the rim, lots of people did that, and did he know the temperature could rise twenty degrees in a few hundred feet, and he wasn't really dressed for that, now was he? The ranger wore sunglasses and a squared-off hat, and she tried to stand in Marcus's way, but she was no more imposing than one of the fat squirrels people fed concession-stand pretzels to, and he pushed past her, grunting, all in a lather, his breath loud in his ears. He wiped the moisture from his brow and upper lip and trudged past in a cloud of his own stink.

He hated women like that, anyway, the skinny ones—hated the tidiness of them, the artificially hairless legs, the white crumbles of deodorant that stuck under their arms, the soft midsections secreting a thousand repulsive hormones and odors and fluids. He wasn't crazy about fat women, either, though he felt more of a bond with them, could swap bulimia jokes, argue the merits of fad dieting. It was men he loved. Thin, fat, athletic, chubby; men of all stripes: hairy and shorn, hippie and Republican, HIV-positive, out-and-prouders, flamboyant theater majors and closeted police officers, lieutenants and generals and commanders, butch and femme, all of them, he loved them with a passion that eclipsed everything else, and he had, a few times, even been loved in return.

But it wasn't enough. He'd increasingly come to believe that he was, in the buff-and-bare world of gay fashion and affectation, superfluous. His sexual encounters were short but surprisingly lusty, and being the man he was, he distrusted the ardor certain men pursued him with, and finally, after thirty-one years, had concluded that he was nothing but a fetish. A fat man. Interchangeable with a dozen other fat, gay men he'd seen with pretty-boy satellites, lackeys that, often as not, had been on Marcus's arm last week at Sister's, Millennium, the G-Room in Chicago. He'd become so hung up on his own objectification that he'd ruined the few meaningful relationships he'd had, accusing his beaus of being embarrassed of him when really it was Marcus who refused to eat out, Marcus who had groceries delivered to his apartment on Twelfth Street, Marcus who looked at the muscular bodies on the internet with a mixture of desire and jealousy. And it was Marcus who carried shame enough for two people in his broad chest; Marcus who, one by one, drove his lovers away.

After fifteen minutes of steady plodding, one sandal in front of the other if only by a few inches, he'd drained his water bottle and had to stop. He didn't sit—to get back up would be too much of a struggle—but he leaned against the far wall to rest in the shade before the next corner exposed him once again to full sun. This part of the trail was heavily populated, and the motion of so many hikers kicked up a dust that blew into Marcus's nose and made him wheeze. The hike would be long, but it was something he'd always dreamed of doing. It ranked right up there with learning to swim and losing the weight. The latter two were pipe dreams, out of the question, but the canyon—upon completion, hiking the canyon would be his greatest feat to date. He pushed himself back to standing, his legs wobbly. *Slowly but surely*, he thought. At the two-mile marker there'd be water and a rest area; after that, the traffic would thin and he'd be able to think. He'd have to conquer more rangers who would want to stop him, to turn him around and point him upward, to deliver him to the graces of the living. But he would not be stopped. One way or another, he would reach the bottom of the canyon.

Ella Walcomb shouldn't have been on the trail, either. So much had gone wrong with her plans that she'd almost given up completely. Four years of training, of lifting weights and downing gelatinous energy drinks, of coupling her three-mile morning run with endurance training in the afternoon; four years of forcing her seventy-two-year-old body into the kind of physical condition she hadn't attained in her pregnant twenties or soccer-mom thirties, not during the empty nest years of her forties when she'd worked long hours at J & G Carpet and picked fights with her husband, Gerald, not when she was diagnosed with high blood pressure and cholesterol at fifty-three, not even when she retired at sixty. She'd run her first mile at sixty-eight, and since then had become stronger, more agile, and more energetic than she'd ever been. She couldn't let all that go to waste, even if her best friend and personal trainer, Jane, had keeled over at the gym and died of a heart attack last month.

Jane had been her partner through the training and more, and they'd even, way back before the kids were born, shared a moment that Ella thought about, sometimes, especially since Gerald had died last year after thirty years of marriage. Ella had been thirty-two and Jane thirty-three, and they'd been drinking merlot on the couch and laughing over a story Ella was telling about her first kiss in third grade, when their faces had been suddenly close and Ella knew, with certainty, that Jane would kiss her. But Jane upset the wine instead, and a few months later married a man Ella had never met, and two years after that, divorced him. She never married again, hardly even managed to date, and though they'd stayed close, there hadn't been another moment. Ella often wondered what might have become of Jane, and herself, for that matter, if they'd have grown up today, when women could hold hands in the middle of Winn Dixie, for goodness' sake, where Ella had seen two of them last week, standing closer than friends ought to. Ella had looked away, ashamed for them. Later she'd realized that she was ashamed of herself. She didn't usually allow herself to tread too deeply into these kinds of thoughts, but, hiking the trail that first day, it'd seemed safer, somehow, with Jane gone.

Ella hadn't wept until the funeral, when she'd looked in on Jane in the casket. Her sorrow hadn't been for her own loss, really, but Jane's—a woman who, last week, could run eight miles, do twenty reps of twelve curls, a woman whose body was taut and powerful . . . and utterly useless. Ella had lost many friends in the past decade, had lost her parents long before that, her husband last year, but she couldn't remember ever feeling so grief-stricken as she did looking at Jane's muscles in the casket.

Now, gazing over the red land, the breezy canyon, the jagged switchbacks ahead of her, she tried to imagine holding

Jane's hand. What it might've felt like, how different it would've been from the times she'd accepted Gerry's hand on vacation in Florida, walking the deck at sunset on a cruise to the Bahamas, the Caribbean, the Keys, or after dinner on their anniversary. What might've become of her, of both of them, if Ella had taken Jane's hand in the grocery store, in the health food aisle between the protein bars and rice cakes? But she hadn't. She hadn't done it, and now, instead, she was hiking the trail in Jane's memory.

They'd intended to be the oldest women to complete the hike from rim to rim. Down to the Colorado River on the Bright Angel Trail, back up the other side on the Kaibab. Twenty-three-point-eight miles across. One thousand, eight hundred, twenty-nine meters deep, a vertical mile. Before she'd left Montgomery, Ella had been interviewed by WSFA, the local news station. Her story, especially with Jane having died so suddenly, was of human interest. "Why this?" the anchor had asked into a microphone, the overhead lights beaming down. "Why the Grand Canyon? Why now?"

To prove that I'm still alive, Ella thought. *To prove it to myself.*

"It's something I've always wanted to do," she said. "I'm going for a record."

Being here, though, was not like she'd expected. She'd read the guide books, the hiking manuals, the travel narratives, but it was the incredible sense of space she hadn't been able to see in pictures. She didn't feel like she was hiking at all, but rather floating downward into an immensity of rock. Her legs were strong, her shoulders relaxed. The perspiration under her arms was familiar, a companion. Above her, the sky was fastened like a lid around the canyon; as she strode downward, the heat crawled up to meet her. Her legs grew dusty to the knees, her hiking boots turned gray. Her body was reliable and strong, if not fast. She had to take frequent breaks. By six o'clock she was still two miles away from Bright Angel campground, and by seven-thirty the light was too low to continue.

She spread her sleeping mat on a flat boulder still warm from the day, then dug a pit in the ground to make a small, inconspicuous fire. She was camping illegally, so she had to be careful. As soon as she'd cooked a few chicken strips in foil, she put out the fire and ate in the dark. Then there was nothing left to do but sleep and hope for a faster day tomorrow, so she removed her pants and put on a white nighty, a garment that was completely inappropriate for the trail but that relaxed her, made her feel at home. The fabric glowed a little, as did the muscle cream she rubbed on her thighs and calves. Her knees ached from the slope of the trail. When she was finished she settled back on her mat, sipping vitamin water and trying to pick out shapes in the dark: a twisty pine tree, jutting projections of granite.

She'd just spotted Zoroaster Temple when she saw him, a beast of a man bumbling down the trail above her. She'd overtaken him two miles earlier, had walked behind him until the path widened enough for her to pass. He'd been struggling then, but now, even through distance and dim light, she could see he was exhausted. He staggered, swerved too close to the edge, skidded over rocks he didn't see. He was moving faster than his body wanted to allow, and in a moment Ella understood why. Behind him, a group of kids—teenagers, Ella thought, because of their dress: baggy everything, shirts, jeans, and shoes—in leisurely pursuit. As she watched, one boy bent, dislodged a stone from the trail, and hurled it at the fat man, catching him in the small of the back. The man arched forward, catching himself on a rock face. Then he ripped a handful of gravel from beneath him and tossed it backward, blindly, over his shoulder. Ella heard laughter, a hiss of s's, growling voices. Ordinarily, she would've stepped forward to help the man. She'd raised teenagers herself, knew how reckless they could be, how they might continue in this manner until something truly awful happened. But there were a lot of them, at least six she could see clearly, and she was not a young woman, and she didn't want to do anything that would jeopardize her hike. She pulled her mat into the brush on the side of the trail, stamped out the last smoking coals. She crouched beside the trail, wishing the fat man luck, hoping the kids would turn around and leave them both in peace.

The AZK crew—four boys, two girls—went to the canyon often. They went to lots of canyons often. And cliffs and bluffs and crevices, anywhere there was a large sheath of rock that looked impossible to get to. The girls carried backpacks filled with paint sticks and rock chisels; the boys wore karabiners and harnesses under their clothes. They were expert at both activities: rock climbing and graffiti. Their destination tonight was the petroglyph above the Colorado River. But they were not above a little violence, and the fat man had gotten in their way.

There was a leader, obvious in the way the others watched him, but they moved as a pack. They considered themselves part of the canyon—their vandalism was an act of deference, of honor. They counted themselves among the Vikings, the vandals of Ancient Greece, to say nothing of the kids in L.A. and Philly, and they were fast becoming notorious as the crew who'd bombed several prominent landmarks in Sedona and Monument Valley. This was their territory—that was why they threw the rocks. Because they valued what was theirs.

"Trespasser," they hissed, sometimes in unison, sometimes echoing each other's whispers like a satanic chorus. They'd each been called that once, twice, in juvenile court or the backseat of a police cruiser, by finger-pointing janitors or highway patrolmen. They'd been honked at on overpasses, spit at on trains, yanked down from the roofs of banks, meat-packing plants, factories.

They'd lived six, twenty, fifty-two weeks in juvie. They'd learned how to climb by doing it wrong. By dangling. Falling. By losing one of their own to a rock-studded chasm on the north rim, twenty miles upriver.

Every once in a while there was a time like this, a moment of payback. The fat man bobbled on the trail, battled it, but the kids didn't stumble once. They allowed the man to gain ground. They toyed with him. The leader, a boy called Juse, plucked a stone from the trail. A perfectly lethal weapon. The leader drew his hand back, over his shoulder (two years ago he'd been a middle school shot-putter), and chucked the stone as far as he could. He missed by a foot—he was not the leader because of his aim; he'd earned the title because of his drawing skills, and because he was the first to climb onto shaky ground and was never, unlike their comrade, the one to fall—but the stone veered into the woods on the other side of the trail and flushed out another victim, an old woman running with her arms over her head.

"Stop," she cried, and the kids did, for a moment. They thought she might be a ranger, and they all knew that their driver—the lanky boy who kept to the back of the group—would lose his car privileges if he got in any more trouble. Two of the others had learners' permits, but not access to a car. The lanky kid, who went by Dex, had his own car, given to him in exchange, as he saw it, for his parents' divorce. But that was his other life. Here, he was the navigator, supplier of gas and cigarettes and, sometimes, beer and weed.

"You've hurt me," the woman said when they hadn't moved. She was ancient, dressed in an old lady nightgown. She looked like a ghost. They'd heard story after nauseating story about the ghosts that inhabited the Grand Canyon, the souls of dead hikers that patrolled the trail after dark. They'd even hoped, in private moments, that they'd see their friend again, the one who'd plummeted down eight stories of redwall limestone. They'd made special trips back to the scene after the police had gone and the trail was re-opened. They'd whispered, each so quietly the others couldn't hear, "Come out."

If they were to see a ghost, they didn't want it to be an old woman in a white dress. After the initial shock of her appearance, one of the kids, a girl called Sifer, pulled out an aerosol can and sprayed a long arrow down the trail. It pointed at the woman. The leader blinked, and the crew moved forward.

Marcus was not dead. He was hurt in places he couldn't see: the back of his shoulder, his left ankle, his tailbone, his ribcage. His round belly stuck out where his shirt had ripped, and it was fine, inconceivably beautiful, unmolested by the thirty seconds of sliding—not falling, he'd never really left the ground—down the cliff. He was oddly energized. He'd given the kids a run for their money, that was sure. Just before he'd taken the wrong step that threw his weight over the edge, he'd clocked one of the boys good with a rock the size of a shoe. He'd taken one out, and he hoped the kid was hurting now, hurting as bad, well, as Marcus was. It'd taken the pain several minutes to enter his system, but now it pounded away in his bloodstream, surging from the cuts on his shoulder down to his busted ankle, and inside, too, in places he couldn't identify.

He had a choice: lie here and wait to be rescued, or heave himself off the ledge he'd landed on and continue downward. It wasn't the ideal spot to jump, by any stretch, but it would finish the job. If he stretched his neck out, he could see that the path to the bottom was a long, straight drop: painless. If the kids hadn't come along, he would've had no doubt about rolling himself over, closing his eyes, and plummeting. It was what he'd been anticipating for weeks, months, ever since the idea had become a concrete plan. But if the kids hadn't come along, he wouldn't have felt that strange desperation to get away, to run, to save himself.

Lying ten feet below the trail, he could see the absurdity of what he'd done. He should've let the kids have their fun, take him out with a wallop to the back of his head. Instead, he'd fought back. The boy he'd hit had gone down, collapsed to his knees, and the others stopped cold, crowding around him. Marcus had taken one step backwards to steady himself, ready to run for freedom. Ludicrous. Now he was stranded on a rock, wondering if it was too late to change his mind.

He shifted onto his side, reached around and touched his shoulder. The blood there was thick, sticky. Things were happening with his body now: clotting, swelling, white blood cells springing into action. All of this seemed wholly apart from him, from Marcus, from how he'd come to think of, to detest, himself. His body went on like a car without a driver. He felt a new affection for it, for all the bodily functions that kept going in spite of his lost will to live. He wondered how long after death they'd persevere—how long after his heart stopped would his stomach keep digesting, his forehead sweating, the minor scrapes on his arm keep trying to heal. There must've been a thin fraction of time when the body lived and died at once. Before the gruesome mess of rigor mortis and cooling and bowel release, things went on as normal. As if death was a simple thing to get through.

But Marcus was not dead, not in any way he could perceive, not yet. And when he saw a face peer over the top of the trail, he knew that he wanted someone to pull him out of there, no matter what the consequences of survival might be.

He cupped his good hand to his mouth. "I'm down here," he yelled, his broken lungs contracting so hard it made his toes curl. "Help me."

Ella remembered only one step from the CPR class she'd taken while the kids were at swimming lessons: survey the scene. Three boys and one girl had taken off, unconcerned, it seemed, about their friends. They'd even stopped to go through her pack, had taken what they wanted from it while Ella pleaded—one boy had struck her in the face when she tried to intervene—then tossed the pack over the edge. The other girl who'd stayed behind now was kneeling over the remaining boy, the one who'd been hit and was lying motionless on the ground. And the fat man was staring up at her from a ledge of rock ten feet below the trail, having toppled over the edge with Ella's bag. The light was gone. They were four miles from the rim.

Ella was stuck. Through all her years of parenting and caregiving, she'd retained a weak stomach, one that recoiled at the sight of injury. She'd been unable to help her son when he'd broken his arm on the playground, had gone to the garbage can and vomited until the ambulance arrived. Even the smallest abrasions made her feel light-headed. She could only imagine what grisly wounds the fat man must've sustained, and the boy would certainly be bleeding, if not worse. She was not the right person to be dealing with this; she'd never been good in an emergency.

Walk away, she thought. *There's nothing you can do.*

She had no bandages, not even the plastic first aid kit filled with Band-Aids and small pieces of gauze she'd kept in her pack. She had no ropes, and even if she did, she couldn't hoist the man up ten feet, even with the help of the two kids, one of whom might be severely injured. She was strong, yes, but not strong enough for that.

Then the man spoke to her, and she knew what she had to do. "Hold tight," she yelled to him.

"No," the man said, and he screamed when Ella pulled her head back. Something fluttered in the brush behind her. She hadn't bothered to pack up the foil from her chicken strips, and the smell would, by now, be drawing the attention of local wildlife. Possibly even dangerous wildlife, bobcats or rattlesnakes. She wasn't prepared for that, either.

She walked to the pair of kids, one prostrate, one crouching. The girl had black hair that was white at the roots. She wore some kind of concert T-shirt and a chain around her waist. Muddy tear streaks lined her cheeks, but she was no longer crying by the time Ella approached. She was scowling at the boy. When Ella was close enough to hear, the girl said, "I think he's dead."

"Is he breathing?" Ella said.

"Yes."

"Then he's not dead."

"Could be."

"No." Ella reached them, bent down over the boy's shoulders. His chest lifted slightly, then fell. His head was tipped to the side and his mouth had fallen open. As Ella watched, a string of drool slipped from his cheek and hung suspended in the air. "He's alive," Ella said. "Unconscious, maybe." She was glad for this. She didn't think she could take an injured, frantic teenager right now. Better that he was knocked out. For a minute, she envied him.

"He could be in a coma," the girl said. "That's as good as dead."

"There's no need to get dramatic." Ella voice had gone firm, the way it often had when her children were in trouble. "Is he your boyfriend?"

"Yeah," the girl said. "But we was going to break up." She put her head on the boy's chest. "I can't hear his heart." She listened with the other ear, then sat up. "He is so dead," she said.

Ella was about to explain how to feel a pulse when the girl reared back and punched the boy in the stomach. Her hand hit with a thud, but the boy didn't move. "Asshole," she yelled. She hit him again. "You fucking fag."

Ella leapt up in horror. She grabbed the girl's arms and tried to pull her away. "What are you doing?" she said.

As Ella struggled with her, the girl kicked the boy, once in the ribs, once in the face. "What does he care," she said.

"He's not dead," Ella said, finally succeeding in dragging the girl away. "And you could hurt him worse."

The girl held up her hands in surrender, and Ella released her. "He had it coming," the girl said. She stepped to the very edge of the trail, a scenic overlook where the canyon dropped straight down to a speck of river. She hung her heels off the edge. "Aren't you going to save me?" she said.

Ella would've rather pushed her. Instead, she turned the boy's head over. She didn't want to, but she had to know how bad it was. She held his chin and rolled his head to the other side. His hair was thick with blood, and there was a brutal indentation above his temple. Ella felt bile rise in her stomach, and she let his head fall back too roughly. It was a severe wound. The fat man had thrown the rock hard, with purpose—he'd thrown to wound. There was blood on the ground.

"What do you mean, he had it coming?" Ella said.

"We found out he done some work for—" the girl eyed Ella—"this gang. He wasn't *loyal*, you know? So, *we* was going to fuck him up. After tonight. All them others thought that fat dude saved us some work." She looked at the boy. "I think he still got some coming."

Ella shivered. She didn't know what the girl meant, exactly, but she believed her.

The girl left the edge and squatted next to Ella. She looked at the bloody ground. "I've got to go," she said. She pointed down the trail. "They're my ride."

"You're not going to help me?" Ella felt stranded, helpless. Old. She didn't know if she could trust her legs to carry her back up to the rim. It'd taken her all day to get here, and that had been downhill in the daylight. If she made it, the rangers might not even listen to her, a decrepit old lady in a white nighty stumbling out of the canyon. She needed this girl. "You're not going to help *him*?" she said.

"He wouldn't have done nothing for me," the girl said, gazing at the boy's face.

"Oh, come on," Ella said, exasperated. "That doesn't matter now."

"Hell, yeah, it does," the girl said. "It matters a lot."

The girl's voice broke. She was tearing up again underneath the makeup and metal, the adolescent bravado. "It sucks," she said to the boy. "But you're not worth losing a ride over."

When she was gone, Ella went back to her camp. It still smelled like chicken. Her sleeping mat was crammed into a prickly bush. She pulled it out, laid it over the boy—he was still breathing. Then she went through his pockets. Clasps, some sort of strap, a bag of tiny pieces of metal. Nothing she could use. She looked over the ledge again where she could barely see the fat man, and farther down spotted the bright red of her bag.

"I'm going for help," she called. "Hang on."

The man didn't respond. She couldn't tell if his hulking shape was moving or not. She was alone. She couldn't even depend on her own body.

"Oh, Jane," she said. She pushed her palms together and closed her eyes. "Help me, Jane."

She'd heard of people having spiritual experiences in times of crisis. But instead of Jane appearing in a ball of light from heaven, an image entered Ella's mind of Jane on her last day alive. She'd been on the step machine, climbing to nowhere, when she'd stopped and bent over her knees like she was out of breath. Ella had been talking about the Grand Canyon.

"We'll need cameras," she'd said. "To document. We could hire a photographer like those women who went through the arctic."

"I don't feel well at all," Jane had said. She'd gone down on one knee, like she was going to propose.

"You've overexerted," Ella said.

"Shoot," Jane said. "I think something's wrong."

Ella had gone for a trainer and on the way had looked in the gym mirror, tucked a strand of hair behind her ear. Congratulated herself on how healthy she'd looked. When she returned, Jane had not been breathing.

It was the *shoot* that Ella couldn't get out of her head, the flippancy of it. *Shoot.* As if it hadn't occurred, even to Jane, how wrong things could go.

Ella opened her eyes and looked at the enormity of the canyon before her. She heard coyotes howling. Somewhere inside were other people, people like her. They'd come for the challenge—they'd come to witness something great. But people always mucked things up. And now Ella, who could've cared less about either the boy or the fat man, had to stand, lift the skirt of her nighty, and climb into the pitch dark canyon.

Shoot, she thought. *And darn. And fiddlesticks.*

Three boys, one girl. That was all they had left. It meant shifts in the routine, equipment changes, a few extra tasks for each kid. But they were going ahead as planned. One of the boys carried an extra backpack from the girl they'd left behind. They were stunned but undeterred. They were used to carrying on in the presence of danger; they were used to acting like nothing had happened.

There had been a scuffle early on when the remaining girl, Outlaw, had wanted to go back for the other. She'd used the other girl's real name—Melissa—which was something they never did. But the leader had calmed her, reminded her that their mission was sacred, that they were going to build a 'piece, and that was that most important thing. Reminded her that if she turned back, she was sure to get picked up by a ranger, or even the police. Had she liked juvie that much, he said, that she wanted to go back? And what if the fat man was dead? She was seventeen, just ripe for being tried as an adult.

She'd gone with them, mutely, through four miles of main trail and then three miles of a roughly cleared path that led to the petroglyph. Once they'd left the Bright Angel, they all felt better. Their night vision was sharp, honed, and they used their senses to navigate more than the pin-lights they carried. Before any other place in the world, before high school or their parents' houses, before football games and concerts and mosh pits, before girls' bathrooms and boys' locker rooms, before bedrooms and borrowed cars, this was where they belonged.

They couldn't see the Colorado until they'd left the ground and were suspended against the limestone wall, their clothes piled at the top, cheeks and soles pressing into the cooling sediment. They rappelled downward until they saw it, a flash of foaming rapids, a muddy, churning field of water that tomorrow would bring canoes and kayaks and guided rafts, but that now only carried residue of rock and bone to the sea. The air was moist and loud. The kids leaned back against the ropes, retrieved the paint from their backpacks. While the leader outlined the piece, the other three tested colors on their arms, small sprays of black, yellow, red, and blue paint they'd stolen from art stores, aerosol cans with caps they used to adjust the spray. They crawled like spiders around the canvas, eyeing it, envisioning it, feeling it out. When the leader was finished, he hung slack in his ropes and howled. The others began filling the blank space he'd carved out.

In moments, they were lost. Inhaling the fumes, their whole bodies absorbed into the effect, knees gripping, straddling, impaling themselves on knife-edged rocks, arms stretched out to the side and over their heads, leaning, arching, they reached for the farthest corners, they swooped up the wall. They gambled limbs, hair, skin for the chance to paint places no one had ever touched. To them, it was as if the images already lurked beneath the rock, and the kids were merely discovering them: letters crawling out like overgrown vines, hands with gnarled fingers and long nails extending outward from within the earth, a hooded grim reaper with purple cape billowing, the eyes of the canyon peering from between rocks, climbers with fevered faces struggling to hold onto their grips. A face with the eyes and the mouth reversed, their group logo. Beyond them all, the angel, black-hole eyes fixed on the river, fire halo circling his head, arms outstretched and pinned to the rock. A heavy metal deity, piercing, earsplitting—the kids heard the furious beat, the dissonant guitar licks, the throaty singer growling into the mike. This was their nirvana, their heaven, and it was angry. They drew life from the rock, set it in motion so that the angel's hair whipped backward in a real wind, the sleeves of his cloak rippled, his chest rose. They heard him scream, felt him rip through the rock, saw him charge at them with bloody teeth. Their bodies shuddered, convulsed, but their hands remained steady. The kids they'd left behind had vanished from their memories.

But the girl was still there. Sitting on the edge of the canyon wall, listening to it erode. Left with the boyfriend who'd cheated on her—cheated on the whole group, but her especially.

She'd gone after her friends, found the place where they'd left the main trail, had wandered for hours, it seemed, trying to find another trace of them. She hadn't gone far when she began to see things. Hear things. She didn't believe in ghosts, but she sure as hell believed in mountain lions. Rattlesnakes. Scorpions.

She'd turned back. The old woman was gone when she reached the part of the trail where her ex-boyfriend was drooling into the dirt. She'd been listening to his breath when she noticed the noises around her. If she listened closely, she thought she could hear animals rotting, plants decomposing. Dinosaur bones embedded in the walls cracked. A sandstone pebble tumbled into the river.

If she turned her head upwind, the girl could smell the faintest odor of spray paint.

The ground, when she sat at the edge, was warm. Underneath her, the earth vibrated. She was not alone. She was abandoned—she'd been dumped, cast off by her so-called friends, by the very people she'd stood up for against her ex-boyfriend—but not alone. She was sure of it. All around her things were breathing and blinking. Underneath, single-celled organisms chewed through cell walls.

Maybe she believed in ghosts a little, after all. But mostly her belief was a hope that if anything *did* exist behind her ex-boyfriend's blank face, it wouldn't appear while she was sitting there. She didn't care whether he was alive or dead—either way, at this point he meant nothing to her, absolutely nothing—except that she didn't want his ghost hanging around to bother her.

Beneath her, tectonic plates shifted and magma rose. Water forced its way through pinholes too small to see and opened them, widened, created space. Pushed a stone loose, and another. One fell at the girl's feet. She stopped, picked it up. She chipped bits of it off with her fingernail. Her knees were in her armpits. There were stones all around her, she saw, hundreds of them, enough to last her all night. Until someone came to take her ex-boyfriend away. She peered over the edge, smiled at what she saw. One by one, she released the stones, dropping them slowly, carefully, tenderly onto the carcass of a fat man.

knock them down

☙

Sometimes she felt like rare jewels—in a bar, sexy-lucky, flirty jokes flying like gunfire—but mostly Dana felt anonymous. Provocatively anonymous, she sometimes consoled herself, anonymous in the fashion of counterculture poets, if she would've possessed the patience for poetry. Even as she lacquered up with colorant, constructed ultrachic features with shadow and highlighter, she worried that while her face and figure caused men to call her intriguing, even enigmatic, her *life* was standard-rate, one of the thousands pumped from the haunches of America. She realized one night, having locked barstools with the same pathetic alchie she'd met last week, that she was pivoting on the place, contenting herself with the inkling of prominence the city issued her, like fatigues. Halfway through her thirties already, she didn't want to sail into mid-life knowing that she had great potential, potential by the barrelful, but potential that could never be realized in Ohio. The solution, then, when it struck her that night, was simple. Leave.

"South?" her friends all said, one by one, "you're really going to move South?"

"Why not?" Dana said. "It's warm. It's sunny. There's a new movie studio."

Four of them were coming out of Studio 58 in Columbus, bumping shoulders and tying limp scarves around their necks. They'd gone to see a *Jaws* festival but had left, disappointed, after the first film. Dana remembered *Jaws* as a chilling antidote to today's proliferation of romantic comedies; but seeing it again, she wasn't chilled at all. She'd actually laughed out loud when the shark first appeared, mechanical and ridiculous. It'd depressed her.

"Why not Hollywood?" one of her friends asked.

Dana told them that Hollywood was over, passé, done: knocked up, left out, married to a banker. *That* done.

"I want the boomtown," she said.

Her friends laughed, bet six months, tops, before she'd be back. Dana said that in six months, they'd be watching her on the previews.

Her plane departed Columbus on the forty-fifth consecutive gray day and descended two hours later into a state steeped in sunshine, the word (beautiful, prodigious) spelled out in bushes next to the runway: *Orlando.* A thump of jubilance struck her chest when she thought of how the other word, *Hollywood,* had swelled into fame—not because of the place, exactly, but because myth and idolatry and zoom lenses threw people into trances, all spinning eyes and empty wallets. *You are getting sleepy,* Dana thought, watching the other passengers prepare to disembark. None of them looked remotely as restless as she felt. *Look into my eyes.*

First class began filing patiently, orderly, out of the plane, but Dana was stuck in a window seat behind the wing and had to remain seated. Her seat mate was straining to dislodge the colossal impedimenta she'd forced into the overhead bin, while her three small children lolloped up and down the aisle. After some struggle, two garment bags crashed to the floor, sideswiping one of the kids. The boy looked surprised for a moment, deciding whether or not the smack of leather hurt enough to wail. Then he wailed.

"Sorry," the mom said to Dana, flashing a smile as toothy as an alligator in a lipstick commercial. She wiped the child's face with her thumb. "You know how it is."

Dana scowled, irritated more at the delay than the noise. The excitement of her decision—such a simple solution, move to Florida—had been condensing into a gym ball in her stomach ever since they'd landed, and it left her feeling rubbery. She looked out the window at the rich, desperate sunlight and decided that once she got off the plane, she'd be okay.

Besides, contrary to the woman's comment, she had no idea how it was. She looked around for a sympathetic shrug, someone else annoyed by unbridled displays of motherhood, but everyone in coach had their own assemblage of children and spouses wriggling around them. Dana was, it seemed, the sole unaccompanied pilgrim of the lot.

"We're all excited to be here," she said loudly. Her words came out sounding panicky, but no one paid her any attention. The mother slung the bags over her shoulder, devoted a finger to each child, and moved her caravan down the aisle. Dana took a deep breath and followed.

Dana's friends, even her parents, attributed her decision to move to another of Dana's eccentric and random gestures. A former theater major, she was known for them. In reality, moving to Florida was the most calculated decision she'd ever made, more deliberate than college, certainly, her only other big decision, where she'd accepted the first cheap, state school that let her in and dropped out two years later when the theater department refused to cast her in any of the school productions. The professors had cited inadequate grades, but Dana believed that her ex-boyfriend, a senior, had effectively blackballed her. She moved back to Columbus and joined the community theater, worked there two months before hearing about Orlando.

Orlando: two new production studios had burgeoned virtually overnight, and a slew of minor celebrities had already been spotted in the Hard Rock Cafe. Newspapers were calling it Hollywood East. As Dana had toured middle schools for the theater's outreach program—*A Midsummer Night's Dream* meets Charlie Brown—the first wave of crews and stars had been flying South, and by the time she'd bowed to the last auditorium of spiteful sixth graders, the studios had produced two major motion pictures. Half the people in her troupe booked flights for the summer, just to see the thing. When the lease on her studio came up for renewal in early May, Dana decided to skip town, beat her cronies to the good jobs. She was fed up with small town commissions. After all, the big opps were for people willing to zip down and win them.

Dana was willing. She packed her push-up bras.

Dana set up camp at the closest Best Western to Lake Buena Vista, which put her within range of both studios, MGM and Universal. She dumped her stuff—all she could fit into a six-pack of luggage—in the room, and changed into jeans and a tube top. The hotel advertised a free shuttle to the theme parks, and while she waited for one to arrive, she bought a *Sentinel* from the machine out front. As she withdrew the paper, a bus sidled up to the curb, releasing a stream of exhaust like a sigh. A dozen toweled children, fresh from the pool, lined up at the behest of a woman with a whistle around her neck. Dana pushed past them and asked the driver where he was headed.

"Resorts," he said, which sounded as good as anything, so she fell in line and chose a seat near the back facing five broad smiles in Speedos and mouse ears. A firing squad of imported delight.

The bus wobbled forward, and the smiles began discussing something in Spanish or Portuguese—Russian, for all Dana could understand. Then the tallest male, the dad, plucked a pair of abandoned mouse ears from the seat next to him and held it out to Dana.

"For you," he said, laughing. All his children wore similar ears, as did he.

Dana frowned, shook her head.

"For fun," he tried, holding the hat in both hands.

"No," Dana said, confused by this game. It didn't just make her uncomfortable, the situation was downright bizarre. The man was still smiling, but looked sinister now. He stood, and Dana braced herself, expecting something crazy. He leaned over and planted the hat on her head, securing it with a pat, then spread his arms in a gesture of *voilà*. He faced the rest of the bus, and said, "Eh?" The driver glanced in his rear-view. A few people clapped.

"Outrageous," Dana said.

The driver, turning back to the road, found a fast-approaching rumble strip and smashed the breaks. Dana pitched face-first into the man. The hat stuck like wax.

"No, thank you," he said, backing away with his hands raised in the air. "Ha ha, no thank you."

Dana peeled away, said, "My stop," and skittered to the front of the bus. The toweled children had started singing Christmas carols though it was almost summer. Dana tried to give the hat to one of them, but the woman with the whistle shook her head. She offered it to the driver as he pulled to a stop.

"No, thank you," he said, pulling the lever that opened the front doors. The children broke into a round of "Deck the Halls." Dana saw the driver laughing as she exited. She threw the hat in the gutter.

The bus's destination, a gaggle of hotels looming behind crew-cut palms, stood in the distance, but Dana could tell by the photo kiosks and uniformed attendants that she was squarely on Disney property. The closest place to sit and read her newspaper was across the street, at a lake studded with beach chairs, and she parked herself at its licking rim. She stretched out on a chaise lounge, pale and lithe in her tube top, looking a little gothic among the plump khakis and skirted bathing suits around her. Flat, plastic sandals everywhere, she noted disdainfully, soles as delicate as the hooves of baby calves.

Dana let a leg hang over each side of the chair, and the lake fondled her toes like a languid courtesan, tired of her duties and growing cruel. Dana felt faintly wicked, the only person around the lake not encapsulated in the throes of monogamy, matrimony, maternity.

Friends swore that someday she'd crave marital bliss, perform the nasty tricks they all did to procure it, but Dana steadily repelled those ideas. Her problem with khakis and sandals was that they reflected, with absolute candor, the insipidity of coupledom: the greed and martyred sex; the bartered *I love you's* and the host of clichés that accompanied them; the intimacy that tarnished, gradually turned to alienation. Dana thought that if the mated majority were going to broadcast their unions, they ought to make them at least *look* pleasant. Then she might be more inclined to join them.

Another thing her friends said, in college, was that she might've been a slut had she ever slept with men. They exaggerated—she'd had boyfriends—but they were right that her attitude didn't match her experience. Dana was willing to be a vixen, hell-bent on becoming one at times, but only when there was no real chance of failure. She played the part right up until the pivotal moment, but then she backed out. In fact, the only sex she'd had was with committed boyfriends, and there had been only four of those. She told people that she was prepared to sleep her way to the top, but until Florida she didn't really expect the opportunity to present itself. Florida, she hoped, would un-inhibit her. Lying scantily clad on a beach full of sexual modesty, she almost believed it would work. She could be the aggressor. She was imagining herself sauntering up to a producer, sliding a hand up his thigh, when an actual man approached her and broke her reverie. He was hairy, wearing bikini briefs and mirrored sunglasses. All confidence ran out of her, of course—what could she expect, so soon?

"Vacationing?" he said.

"Just moved here," she returned, trying to appear casual. "I'm an actor."

"Aw, that's great." He extended a hand. "Reeves."

"Dana," she said. "One en." They chuckled together, Dana trying desperately to avoid looking at his wiggling, too-tight suit, an endeavor which painfully backfired. All that vestigial hair; all that bulge.

"Well, Dana," he said, drawing out the name like venom through a syringe, "I own a business myself. And if you don't give me a call, I will be very disappointed." He laughed again, and Dana shrunk back. *The jiggle,* she thought, *my god, the jiggle!*

"I hire actors," he continued. "There are people to whom I could introduce you."

Dana accepted his wink and his card, trying to decide if she'd met a mogul or a pimp. "There are people"?

"That's so nice," she said stupidly. "I'll do that."

"Do that." He eased back onto the chair. "Would you feel that sun? Superb." As if the weather had been served up according to his personal taste.

They fell silent, and Dana closed her eyes behind her sunglasses. Just for a moment, she told herself, sinking back into the chair. When she woke later, Reeves and his briefs were gone.

She didn't know how much time had passed—the sun seemed to drift randomly about the sky, never moving in the direction she expected—but she'd developed a nasty burn. She twisted her head around to see how her shoulders had fared. Their color had deepened so much that if they hadn't been *on* her, she might not have recognized them. She moved to an isolated spot under an umbrella but was soon disturbed again, this time by an attendant. He was decked out in a red polo with the Disney logo embroidered on his chest, and an apron in the style of concession stands and hardware-store clerks. He informed her that the posh, shaded spots cost ten dollars an hour, which would be a hefty chunk of Dana's funds. She'd brought the cash from her last paycheck with her, but she didn't have much to spare; she'd planned to start working right away. Still, after a moment's deliberation, the cushy seat won out over prudence.

"That's damn expensive UV protection," she told the boy, trying to recover the smarts she'd lost to Reeves. She handed over a twenty, practiced her strategy. "Think that buys me enough time to find a job?"

"Depends on the job," the boy said. She was smiling up at him—he was cute, in a youthful, rangy way—but he deposited the money, marked a card, and with a final "Happy hunting," loped off. That made three men today—mouse ears, Reeves, and this boy—who weren't the least bit fazed by the good looks that had gotten her so much attention in Ohio. Dana reached for the Classifieds again, attributing their disinclination to her own coolness, the fact that they'd taken her off guard. She didn't need to reevaluate herself, just adjust her expectations.

After she'd circled a few ads, Dana dozed off again, weary from the travel and the intense sun. She woke periodically to the sounds of children racing the shore, slathered in sun screen, their mothers sliding silently into the water.

That night, after bathing in the rust-ringed hotel shower and lathering her burn in aloe, Dana took a cab to Pleasure Island in search of good luck. She was ready to devastate in slinky pants and a halter top, and she trusted that her pink shoulders would appear charming in dim light. On the dance floor, she hurled men against her like a seagull dropping shellfish on the rocks, snuffling for the bit of treasure they might contain. She swung her hair and her hips, tried to pry her partners open without getting too close. Some were helpful; others just confused her.

"You know how to dance?" one asked, when she mentioned job-hunting. She laughed, because they *were* dancing. He said, "I mean, really dance."

"Seven years tap and modern," she said. "But that's not what I want to do."

"Doesn't matter," he retorted. He gave her a knowing look. "It's what they want you to do." He said it so profoundly, Dana almost thought it made sense.

"They?"

"You'll see."

They went to the bar, and Dana ordered a shot of whiskey. Not her normal drink, but she was feeling wild, acutely undomesticated. Fifteen minutes later, the bartender returned with a fluted glass, brimming pink and ringed in fruit slices. Dana giggled, and held the glass in the air.

"That," she told her partner, "is the prom queen of whiskey shots. Dressed up and ready to get laid." She watched his reaction.

"It looks like a maid of honor," he said.

At the next club—country-western—a bulky man tinged green with exhaustion collapsed on the stool beside her. She'd watched this hulk try to line dance for twenty minutes, never accomplishing more than the odd knee slap, a pendulum swing of the foot. He caught her gaze, mistook her smirk for an advance.

"Where are you from?" he asked, gulping a beer.

"Ohio. Corn capital of the world."

"I thought that was Iowa. Des Moines, here. Nice to meet you."

She took his hand and looked into his face. He was a vast man, ample in both girth and mental desolation, she could see that. His eyes looked like they might be hollow. The perfect specimen.

He said, "You look like you need to be seduced, Ohio."

Dana twinkled. "Well," she countered, "seduce, then."

He walked two fingers like massive quarter rolls up her leg. "I don't even want to know why you're here," he said.

Dana hadn't heard that particular line before, but she had to admit it was sexy. It obliterated the need for small talk (what do you do, who do you like, have you been tested) and allowed their speech to veer into one-liners and weird facts, truths Dana didn't know she knew or cared about. It was as if they passed through a whole relationship, all the things held back or doled out over time, in the span of an hour.

"I'm going to be famous," she told him.

"I'm going to have another beer," he said, and did.

Then later, "I'm good enough to be famous."

"Doesn't matter. As long as you don't have any morals."

And, after another drink, "Fear. That's my morals. That's what keeps me in line."

"Good enough," he said. Then, "Marry me."

"Think again," Dana said.

She took his hand and led him to a booth where he sat next to her and mauled her with his lips. She let him suck and grope, no fear, no fear at all, but after a few minutes he pulled completely away.

"I don't know what's wrong with me," he said, holding his head. "That last beer . . ."

Dana sighed, slid under the table. She crawled to the other side, away from him.

"Some other time," she said.

"Nice meeting you." He rubbed a blister of her saliva off his chin. That was all it came down to in the end: a bit of drool and a spinning head. Dana left the Island.

The next day things started to hit. The excitement of the night before surrendered to the attrition of morning, joblessness. Dana answered two ads for dancers, remembering the premonition of the guy in the club, but it turned out he didn't have a clue—she didn't get either job. One required extensive knowledge of ballet, the other donning one of many mouse, dog, or duck costumes, all over thirty pounds, with air-conditioned heads. Dana went as far as trying on the grinning duck suit-she needed the money—but the humiliation, when she glimpsed her reflection in a window, was too much. She understood about starting at the bottom, working her way up, but she had limits. She didn't even fill out the torso; it hung loose around the wings, and her bare legs stuck out like blunt needles from the egg body.

Dana went back to the Classifieds, and the next afternoon, her third day, she got an audition. Actually, the auditions were open, one day only, and she had to take a cab across town and wait in a long line to be seen. Universal Studios was hiring faux street performers, people who would stroll the streets of fake New

York and phony Paris, entertaining very real crowds. There were jugglers, snake handlers, celebrity look-alikes. Dana performed a monologue. She didn't even make the first callback.

That night she fished the number from her bag—still sandy— and called Reeves. His secretary told her to come by in the morning for orientation.

"It's a good job for actors, right?" she asked.

"Sure, hon. Actors, directors, producers. Whoever."

She went to the orientation, but only because she needed the money worse with every night she spent in the hotel. Plus, she told herself, any indignity she had to suffer was only temporary. Everyone had to wallow in shit awhile; nothing personal. She wasn't entirely optimistic, but she admitted that Reeves's offer might be legitimate. Hadn't he promised to introduce her to people?

What Dana didn't know, what she'd learn later, was that every eight minutes, in any part of the city, a hired kid from Park Services swept any trash—gum wrapper or bird crap—into a dust pan on a handle, left the streets looking like peace on earth. She wanted to be raunchy and mean; they wanted her to wear a duck suit and hug sweaty children. She just didn't fit the part.

At eight A.M. sharp, Dana found her trainer, Pietra, at a kiosk in the Outlet Mall underneath a sign that read, "Free Disney Tickets." Dana made a joke about the greater hazards of trying to confine Disney tickets, but Pietra gave her a blank look. Dana understood why as soon as Pietra spoke: she'd been in the country over a year, but didn't have the language under control yet. The object of the game, Pietra explained with some difficulty, was to lure tourists to the kiosk with theme-park promises, whisk them away to a "tour" of Deer Creek: An Ideal Living Community, and then badger them into buying a canal-front piece of land. Dana got them interested, Pietra drove the van. Upon returning from the "tour," the "—ists," as Dana began calling them, received a pair of standard Magic Kingdom tickets, enough to get them on

the Dumbo ride but not much else. The business ran like orga-
nized crime, Dana packing in the cargo and Pietra piloting them
away. After a few hours, Dana forgot that all they were smuggling
was an assortment of gullible vacationers, and the only place they
went was back and forth to a drained swamp trimmed with a couple of model homes. The details of the place were so clandestine,
it felt like they dealt in illegals.

Between deals, the women chatted, and Pietra mentioned
that she was a part-time actor.

"An actor," Dana said. "Like me."

"Sisters," Pietra breathed.

"Single?"

"In general."

Pietra had moved to the U.S. from Italy to become an actor,
refusing to let a little thing like the language barrier bother her.
She seemed to be doing quite well, in fact, working seasonal
jobs around town, and returning to Deer Creek in the off-
season. She listed her various roles, all nonspeaking parts, in
broken English, pausing over a haunted amusement park she'd
worked last Halloween.

"A fabulous job," she told Dana. "For the actors. I hook you
up this year."

Normally actors worked the live ghost routine—strolling
around in bloody clothes or with chain saws, jumping from
behind trees, Dana knew the type—but Pietra had won one of
the park's singular positions, the one they advertised as a must-
see. She was Rat Woman. The job consisted of lying partially
clothed in a glass coffin that teemed with live rats.

"And people pay to see this?" Dana asked, delightfully
horrified.

"Oh, yes. They love it."

Pietra had not always had it so well, though, as she explained
to Dana. She'd arrived from Parma on the cusp of an unknown

pregnancy, and couldn't get anything other than positions in ticket sales. Once her stomach inflated, things changed. She began getting all the good gigs. Dana was incredulous, but Pietra insisted that it was true. Apparently, she hadn't ballooned out until the last two months, just got fuller in the breasts and abdomen, and acquired a motherly glow—she called it "my mama red"—that was a hit in the live (nonspeaking) performance circuit. She'd met Reeves shortly before giving birth, when he'd approached her much the same way he'd recruited Dana. Pietra and Reeves's wife had gotten along famously, and Reeves and the wife had supported Pietra through the delivery of a baby boy with black hair and dimpled fingers—she showed Dana the pictures. Dana recognized Reeves's roomy smile in the picture, next to the hospital bed; on the other side, his wife poured champagne. Dana remarked that it must've been hard raising a child all alone in a foreign country, but Pietra said no, she'd had more support now than ever before. Even so, Dana pitied the girl: she was young and plump, had nothing on Dana's good looks, and a kid to boot. She'd never make it.

Two weeks later, Pietra announced she'd taken a new job as Snow White in the Electric Parade and would be leaving Deer Creek.

"I am fairy tale," she told Dana.

Dana was glad to see her go. Pietra had been making comments about Dana's performance lately, saying she had bad technique. Dana had informed her that she best stick with rats, and their relationship, what small one they'd formed, had deteriorated ever since.

Reeves blew in the next day, looking almost handsome in tan pants and a flowered shirt. It was the first time Dana had seen him since the beach.

"There she is," he said to no one, "the only girl who fell asleep *before* I started talking about my job."

Dana didn't have time to apologize because almost in the same breath, he snagged a couple of —ists wandering by. They worked steadily until lunch, and then Reeves disappeared for an hour. When he returned, he had a woman on his arm, tall and matronly, sheath of hair curling delicately around minuscule ears. The woman disappeared into the bathroom while Reeves joined Dana.

"Who's the skirt?" she asked.

"What?" he said, but the woman wafted back out of the bathroom then, freshly layered in cranberry lipstick, and Dana recognized her face from Pietra's picture. She had cheeks so perfectly round they looked like implanted Superballs. "Right," Reeves said, catching her hand. "Dana, meet Brigid, my wife. I thought we could use the help."

"Of course," Dana said, pleased to get a close-up of Pietra's benefactress.

"I hope you don't mind," Brigid said, throwing a tolerant smile at Dana. Dana could feel the woman sizing her up. "Reeves is going to interview some potential applicants."

"Of course," Dana said again. She knew Reeves's interviewing process. The thought of him cozying up to some twenty-year-old made her think of Pietra again, and Dana was suddenly sorry she'd not been nicer to the girl. Pietra, after all, had no hope of totally escaping Reeves. After Snow White, she'd be back at Deer Creek. Dana wouldn't be surprised if they had some illicit arrangement on the side.

Reeves appeared and disappeared throughout the day, gassing up on kisses from his wife between interviews. Dana found it disgusting. It was a slow afternoon, and when he was gone, by way of conversation, she mentioned Pietra's new job. Brigid perked up like a cocker spaniel. She told Dana that she'd orchestrated it—she had some clout in the theme park—so that when the current Snow White went back to college in Vermont, the job went straight to Pietra.

"We wanted to keep her around," Brigid said. "She's part of the family. We don't have children of our own. And this parade job will be great for her career." She paused for emphasis and said, "She's from Italy, you know."

At the end of the day, while Brigid closed the kiosk, Dana pulled Reeves aside to remind him of the connections he'd vowed to toss her way. She was afraid he'd disappear for another two weeks, leaving her without any possibilities.

"Yeah, sure," he said. "I meant to tell you. Tomorrow night. Big party at Deer Creek—one of the *Die Hards*—plenty of contacts. Brigid knows some people in the business."

"*Die Hard*?" Dana said. "As in, Bruce Willis?"

"Come, why don't you."

Dana nodded, delirious with gratitude. Her chance. "I'll be there."

"Nine o'clock. It's the first model, you'll see it." Brigid interrupted him with a discrepancy between the roster and the log, and he turned away, leaving Dana shivering in expectation.

The house rested in mud, and mud surrounded it in every direction, a platform upon which the structures looked like objects in a crude vaudeville show. Dana supposed one could call the runoff streaming through tire tracks a "creek," but nary a deer would skip pencil-legged through this place. It was undeveloped, to say the least. As far as ideal living communities went, Dana could think of no location more unsuited to the name. The sign outside, spotlighted and garnished with blooming hibiscus, only made the desolation within more, well, desolate. Dana picked her way across the bog that was the front yard and placed her pumps atop the pile of soiled boots and loafers outside the front door. The skirt she was wearing, a long one, iridescently red, had been defiled by mud on the trip to the front door. She'd done her hair in ringlets—a *Glamour* tip for standing out at a party—and, at the advice of the saleswoman in the mall, had bought and worn an actual bustier. She'd spent a fortune on the outfit, the last of her cash and all her profits from Reeves combined.

The man who greeted her at the door had the white pantsuit and sunglasses that earmarked, without a doubt, the traditional Elvis costume. Dana got a sinking feeling.

"Don't tell me," Elvis said. "Scarlett O'Hara."

Dana looked down at her soiled skirt and nodded, sadly. "Fiddle-dee-dee," she said.

"The hair," he said, as if that explained everything.

Dana entered the hallway feeling silly in muddy clothes and bare feet, not at all the image she wanted to project this night. The other guests were drinking cocktails in the living room, dressed in the stock characters one would expect to find, from Cher to Judy Garland, and Dana spent most of her time trying to decide which were celebrities, which were celebrity look-alikes, and which were celebrities dressed as other celebrities. She kept seeing familiar faces—at one point she was sure she saw Pietra—but they would turn out to be strangers, or, like Pietra, complete mirages. The host and hostess breezed in and out, stopping only to offer her the most nebulous remarks.

"Dana," Brigid beamed. "So glad."

Later Reeves touched her shoulder. "Finding your way around the room?"

Dana was not, in fact, finding her way anywhere but to the platter of shrimp on the coffee table, but Reeves seemed not to care. She could tell by the way he clung to the back of the couch that he was quite drunk. She'd attempted to make conversation a few times, but had given up when the conversation moved no further than her amazing Scarlett costume. She was fueling up on puff pastries, ready for a second round of connection-making, when Elvis sat beside her on the couch.

"Scarlett," he cried, opening his arms as if to embrace her. She must've looked surprised because then he explained, "It's the Elvis costume. Makes me feel radical. All that hip swinging."

Dana laughed, relaxed a little. "Are you with the bride or groom?"

"Neither," he said, taking a pastry and licking it. "I'm in casting."

"Really!" Dana smiled big. She lowered her glass and put a hand on his leg. "Well then," she said, affecting a Southern accent, "I've been here three long weeks lookin' for you. I'm an actor, and the only work I've found is either in an animal suit or out here—" she indicated the sweep of the Creek—"on the farm."

"Oh no, I don't have anything to do with that. I'm not actually in *casting*. I'm interning in the studio, that's all. Barely got the job myself."

Dana slumped back against the couch, any idea of making connections hopelessly gone. She'd failed, and failed miserably. She was stuck selling bogus property, and she was broke. She couldn't sleep her way to the top because she couldn't even figure out where the top was. It kept shifting.

"I should have gone to Hollywood," she said.

"What's there?"

Dana thought. "I don't know," she said finally. And she didn't. She didn't know what was in Hollywood, just like she didn't know if it mattered that she was any good at acting. Look at Pietra, making it big without saying a word. As Rat Woman, as Snow White, she was somebody. Dana was no one. An accidental Scarlett O'Hara.

Dana went skidding through the remainder of the night, the farce of romanticism abandoned. She joined mundane conversations and made bad puns; she spilled her drink and crashed into furniture.

"The problem with Scarlett," she announced once to the room, "is that she was a codependent at heart. She needed men, marriage, babies. The whole institution."

The people around her snickered. She stood alone.

At last Elvis offered to drive her home, and she agreed on the condition that he allow her to visit the bathroom first.

"This may be my only chance to pee in the same toilet as Bruce Willis," she told him. He said he'd wait in the car.

Dana had to travel through three or four rooms—she was a little tipsy and lost count—before she found a bathroom. In one of them she saw Reeves, passed out on his stomach. She hurried away, opening and closing doors until she found one with a toilet. Afterwards, she had just as much trouble getting out as she did getting in. She made so many wrong turns, that when she opened a door to find people behind it, she almost didn't notice, probably would've slammed the door quickly—another wrong turn—if the it hadn't uncovered the surprised face of Pietra. No mistaking her this time. She was partially sunk in a bed, naked, though she made no move to hide herself. Brigid was the one who scrambled for cover.

"We are here," Pietra warned, as if she'd had the bathroom door opened on her. Dana registered the scene—Brigid, Pietra, the bunched up bed—in choppy fragments, like a skipping record. She held onto the door frame.

"Who is it?" Pietra called, blinking blindly into the light behind the door.

Dana had a moment, before Pietra's eyes adjusted, when she could see the couple as if behind one-way glass. The blood that rushed out of Brigid's face at being caught seemed to enter into

Pietra, congealing in her nipples. Nothing of the pregnancy showed, except the rosy glow and a wetness at her breast. With Brigid on the floor, Pietra filled the bed. She snapped her jaws at the shadow in the door and smirked, a provocative threat. Dana faltered, felt herself bleed into focus.

"Nobody," Dana said, and shut the door.

In a few weeks Dana was on stage. Elvis—whose name was Ed Banks—had family who worked at Disney, and he set her up with a dance corps that performed live in the amphitheater. Dancing: the prophesy come true, though Dana didn't really know what that meant. It was an in. Ed Banks said it would give her valuable exposure. The dress was modest, but human—no bear wear. When the piped-in synthesizer music began its rumbling the first evening, she flashed a bleached smile to a crowd that pushed all the way back to Tomorrow Land.

For weeks she dazzled in perfect unison with her group, skipping across the stage and kicking up a leg to reveal a demure strip of crotch. Every night, the audience applauded, and the popping flashbulbs made Dana shiver. She saw Brigid's flawless hair speckled throughout the crowd, swinging in the faces of mothers as they bent to collect their families. She danced her way off-stage as a dozen animal suits cartwheeled on, their furry heads nearly decking her every time.

Then, as she disrobed one evening in the underground costume lab, she saw her. The paraders marched out, Pietra queen among them.

"Snow White!" Dana called.

"What?"

"White!"

Pietra blazed a smile of adulation at her, forgetting, as befitted a fairy tale, their past disputes. "Of course," she mispronounced. "From the ticket stand."

She wore a short brunette wig that fell over her forehead, and a gown pricked with tiny lights. In her hands lay a basket of candy to toss at salivating children. Her lips were red as a poison apple.

"We still do the scare job," she said, beginning to move away with the crowd. "Halloween. We still knock them down."

"Dead," Dana said, but the crowd had swallowed her up.

heat rises

We took a two-lane highway through Florida, Kerouac-style, Charlie said, the road less traveled and all that. So when the Suburban overheated on the way to Miami, between nowhere and nothing, we pulled over to a deserted beach with no amenities—not even a parking lot, let alone a boardwalk or beer stand—to cool off. We were halfway into Spring Break, halfway through Florida. We'd passed at least a dozen of these sandy outcroppings, and though we were hoping for something trendier, more MTV, this one—what Steve quickly dubbed Survivor Beach—would suffice for the day.

"*One* day," Jen said, folding her arms over her chest.

"It's like camp," Steve said. "Come on, it'll be so Melrose Place."

Jen shot him a mean look. Steve was the ironic one; Jen was not. He turned to me. "Liz, right?"

"It's better than being stuck at a service station," I said.

Zippy, who was driving, cruised over the dune and down to the water. Me, Jen, Charlie, and Steve unloaded the trunk while Zippy stuck his fingers in risky places under the hood. When we opened the doors, the heat hit us like a horror movie. By the time we'd unloaded the towels and CD players, the boogie boards, the SPFs four, ten, and twenty, Steve's inflatable inner tube, Zippy's water shoes, the Styrofoam cooler filled with Diet Cokes and Dos Equis, the boom box and the beach chairs, we were damn near to exhaustion.

At first, I thought the weather was normal. A typical Florida heat wave. *Of course* it felt extreme to us: we'd just emerged from six months of the worst winter Ohio had witnessed in twenty years, snow piled up to our second-floor dorms, wind that forced our eyes closed. And *of course* it seemed scary: our poor, pale bodies had been buried beneath the Midwestern gray for so long that they'd lost the ability to process sunlight, warmth. Back in December, desperate, we'd made reservations at a cheesy place in Miami called South Seas, where the weight room was Nautilus and the pool had two slides. The pool had been a selling point for Jen: it gave you all the benefits of the ocean without any of the hazards, which she defined as sharks, riptides, syringes, and kids in diapers playing in the shallows. Now she eyed the ocean dubiously, planted her bikinied butt on a beach towel, and misted herself with coconut oil. Charlie and Steve ogled her, and Zippy shouted obscenities from under the hood. I stripped off the clothes I was wearing over my one-piece Speedo and walked toward the water.

The sand was scalding. In the absence of clouds, the searing sun poured over my shoulders and my scalp. I tiptoed to avoid much contact with the sand. I felt my hair turn brittle, my freckles expand. The heat dried out everything, my mouth, my nose, the corners of my eyes. The water before me looked good enough to drink. I licked my lips. If I'd been wearing my heart rate monitor, like I was supposed to, I was sure my pulse would've been racing. I was what doctors called a product of my culture. Overweight, check. Borderline diabetic, check. Asthmatic, check. Allergic to: pollen, check; mold, check; penicillin, check. High blood pressure—at my age?—check.

Flat as a lake, the ocean smelled vinegary. The sun glinted off pockets of whiteness on the surface, but it wasn't until I got right up to the water's edge that I realized they were the bellies of dead fish, which floated all the time in the pseudo-beach we had up in Ohio, but which I hadn't expected to see here. Some were small, some long as my arm. I tested the water with one foot, then jumped backwards. *No way*, I thought, almost ready to laugh. *No freaking way.*

I walked back to the group, where Zippy was saying, "It's completely dead. I mean, the engine won't even turn over."

Jen looked up to adjust her bikini lines. "Hey," she said when she saw me. "Is the water nice?"

"No," I said. "It's not nice at all." I plopped down on a towel and picked up the foot I'd stuck in the ocean. The sole gleamed red, hot skin beginning to blister.

"What, is it warm?" Steve said.

"Worse," I said. "It's hot."

Jen stared at my foot. "How hot?" she said.

I couldn't lie. "Hot enough to kill fish," I said.

Everyone grew silent, except Steve, who laughed.

We gleaned enough from news radio to know that, one, all the snipers and terrorists and war criminals and militants who'd been at it yesterday still were, and two, most of the Southern states were suffering from a heat wave of unprecedented intensity. The National Weather Service had issued an advisory to stay indoors, a sort of Heat Watch they didn't have a siren for. Disaster Relief Squads set up camp on Florida interstates to facilitate evacuation, should it become necessary, and to turn away anyone who tried to cross the border.

"Good thing we left last night," Charlie said. "We might not have made it."

We listened a while longer, but before long, Jen's boom box crackled and went dead. When she opened the back, the batteries were sweating, water droplets beading up on the metal nubs.

The only shelters we had were the car and a group of stunted scrub trees back by the dune. We chose the trees. When we shook off the towels to move them, the sand felt like sparks.

"It's weird," Steve said. "It feels like the heat's coming from the ground."

"Radiation," Charlie, a biology major, said. "It comes from the atmosphere, but gets reflected off the earth."

"Or maybe the ocean is heating up," I said. "Like a hot tub."

"The ocean isn't a hot tub," Charlie said.

But Steve was right: the heat did seem to be coming bottom up. The sun had shrunk to a cigarette burn in the sky. The air itself was blazing, filtering upward in visible waves and distorting our vision. Steve took pictures with a digital camera, kneeling by one of the trees to get a shot of a lizard with a red throat, trekking down to photograph the dead fish. He carried the camera under his shirt so it wouldn't go the way of Jen's stereo. He was an art major who'd spent a semester photographing ecological refugees in the Sudan, snapping black and white shots of hooded women in the desert, children with stick arms and legs eating sand. He'd won cash prizes for two of them and had used the money to buy the digital camera. The pictures were hanging over a gas fireplace in the school's Study Abroad building.

His precautions didn't matter. The heat warped the pictures, and then the shutter jammed and the whole thing blanked out. He returned looking dejected.

"Lockjaw," he said. "Five hundred bucks down the tube."

Charlie started to respond, then stopped short. "You guys," he said after a long pause. "Look at the car."

Zippy's head whipped around. Steve dropped the camera, and Jen lifted her sunglasses. I stood up and shielded my eyes. The car was tilting at an odd angle, as if the back half was sinking. Nobody wanted to move, but if something was happening to the car, we all needed to see.

Shoes flew on, and Steve—like a queen, the fairest of us all— wrapped a towel around his head. He was the first to reach the car, and he pointed to the left rear tire where some sort of black liquid was oozing out, clotting in the sand like blood.

"A leak?" I said, but no one answered. Steve dug around the tire with his shoe, and then I could see that it wasn't a leak at all. Sitting in the sun this whole time, on that scalding sand, the tire had begun to melt. Zippy ran around to the driver's side, twisted the keys hard into the ignition, and pumped the gas audibly. Nothing. No tick, no gurgle. In seconds he had to get out again; the seats were liquefying, turning into vinyl sludge. He began to hyperventilate.

"Calm down, dude," Charlie said. He held his hands low, like he was keeping our nerves under control. "Tomorrow we'll hike into town and find a mechanic. Let's enjoy today. We wanted sunshine, right? We wanted heat."

I touched Zippy's shoulder, which was clammy and red. "It'll be okay," I said. "This probably happens here all the time."

We walked back to the shade, wincing as waves of heat seeped upward through our shoes.

Everybody had a theory. Jen said nuclear holocaust. Steve said second coming. Zippy said apocalypse. But they said these things with a raised eyebrow, a wink. We were desensitized to scare tactics, wary of exaggeration—too ironic to believe in unempirical explanations, too jaded to believe in scientific ones. If we didn't have an answer for what was happening right now, we believed that when we were back in our dorm rooms or loft apartments, parked in front of the tube with a Mountain Dew or a double mocha, watching Fox News or Entertainment Television, then we would understand what had happened. We would point at the screen like people did after hurricanes or tornadoes or floods and, with a sense of real accomplishment, say, *We survived that.*

Right now, we determined, the best thing was to sit tight. Waiting was the one thing we were all good at. We'd had a lot of practice waiting in line and waiting on hold; waiting to turn sixteen, eighteen, twenty-one. We'd been put on waiting lists and in waiting rooms; we waited for our ships to come in and for the other shoe to drop. We waited for test results: to see if we were, or had gotten someone else, pregnant; if we'd contracted or given an STD; if we were over or under the legal limit. We waited to hear the new CD, to see the fall line-up. We waited for field goals and free throws and sudden death shots. We waited for the drugs to take effect. We waited for our mothers to sober up, our fathers to come home.

If we waited long enough, we had no doubt that someone would rescue us.

Jen said meteor crash. Steve said aliens. I said global warming, and everybody got quiet.

"Global warming is real," Charlie said. "It's, like, a fact."

I imagined all the aerosol spray cans in the world being dispensed, miraculously, at the same moment; all the air conditioners and hair dryers and lawn mowers I'd ever used, the smog-pumping cars I'd driven, the fossil fuel-driven airplanes I'd ridden, all of them pulsing heat at once, pushing the boiling point until, with a single turn of the ignition—the proverbial straw—it all came raining back to earth. All those greenhouse gases, accumulating in the sky. I thought of smokestacks and incinerators, those horrible film strip images they show you in earth science class: raw sewage churning, nets heavy with malformed fish. Something about carbon dioxide and heat. Something about trapped energy.

I wondered about combustibility: the beers in their bottles, the gas inside Zippy's car. The blood in my veins.

"So," I said, trying to sound casual. "Spontaneous combustion. That's not real, right?"

"You're looking at what's real," Steve said. "What do you think?"

We'd been on the beach thirty-one hours when I noticed a new sound: the grumble of an approaching storm. Everyone else was asleep, piled limb-on-limb under the trees, reeking of perspiration and the insect repellant that Steve had sprayed on everyone. I woke with my face in Zippy's dreadlocks. The air was so thick it made my lungs ache, but I felt a great sense of relief: a storm would cool things off. I held my hand over the sand—still scalding. Beneath the bug spray smell was the odor of the five of us, the rancid smell of unwashed hair, the baked-in stench of cigarettes. We had more Marlboros than food. We'd planned to gorge ourselves on Cuban pork in Miami, so all we had in the car was an uncooked hotdog, ketchup and pepper packets, and half a McDonald's fish sandwich left over from Jen's value meal. We were hungrier than we'd ever been. Looking at the sand all around me, I understood for the first time what it was like not to care what filled my stomach, as long as something did.

I put on sandals and dug through the cooler for a Dos Equis. It was hot as freshly brewed coffee.

The night was overcast, no stars but a haze of moon streaking through wooly clouds, and bugs so bad I inhaled some with every breath. Despite the bug spray, gnats were everywhere, like the sand itself, irritating skin that was already raw and overexposed. Several feet away, the Suburban glowed, its whiteness almost florescent. It seemed ominous, flatlined in the middle of the beach like that. I gingerly stepped toward it, hoping to find something between the seats that I could eat, something in the glove compartment to take the edge off. I had the gummy feeling in my mouth that meant my blood sugar had plummeted. As I walked, a flash of lightning spread through the clouds, illuminating the beach long enough for me to notice something solid taking shape in the ocean, crawling away from the swash like a detached wave. I waited, everything around me heavy and tingling, then lightning struck again, closer, and I could see the jagged bolt clearly, the way it sent electrified feelers in every direction. The hairs on my arms and in my ears pricked up. An unsteadiness hung in the air, a static charge, like molecules reversing or atoms turning inside out, and then the thunder clap came like detonation. Behind the laborious progress of the first animal—a sea turtle or a seal, I wouldn't have known the difference—three more sloshed free of the water, dragged and heaved themselves upshore.

Everyone was awake and bug-eyed when I returned to camp, empty-handed. Steve was muttering something about heat lightning, Charlie was telling him it didn't exist, Jen was silent, and Zippy was quoting Bible verses. I couldn't tell if he was serious or not.

"I saw Satan fall like lightning from heaven," he said. "The earth watched and trembled."

"Can it, Zippy," Steve said. "I'm telling you. This happens out west every summer."

"Lightning comes from friction," Charlie said. "Not heat."

"Have you ever been in heat like this?" Steve said.

We looked over the water at the light show, bursts coming steady as fireworks, illuminating the creatures crawling from the sea.

"Wherever it comes from," Jen said, "it's making that shit come out of the water. And I'm not sitting here to wait for it." She put on her shoes, gathered a towel around her. Charlie stood, too, and lifted the cooler into his arms.

"Besides," he said. "You're supposed to avoid trees in a storm."

One by one, we trekked back to the Suburban. Zippy forgot about the seats and got a nasty burn when he plopped down on one—it coated the back of his legs with hot plastic that wouldn't peel off. We found that if we layered our towels, left the doors open, and situated our limbs very carefully, we could relax, if not sleep. I finished the Dos Equis, and, situated in the back seat between Jen and Zippy, reached for another. Charlie pulled a baggie of pot out of his pocket and offered some to Zippy. Zippy took a long hit, then passed the joint to me.

"It's kind of like a slumber party," Charlie said, and Jen rolled her eyes. Back in the car, I felt almost normal again. I found a bag of pretzels under the floor mat, and Steve found half a gooey Payday stuck in the visor. Jen put on her sunglasses, even though it was dark. We smoked and drank for hours, heads dropping to each other's shoulders—Jen's legs across three laps, two pairs of arms around Zippy—and after we'd smoked most of Charlie's pot, rolling it into two cigar-thick joints, it really did seem like we were watching fireworks. We ooo-ed and ahh-ed, inhaled deeply and blew the excess out the window. We joked about getting the mosquitoes high and dared each other to run down to the water and touch one of those seal-sea turtle things, ride one, *bring it back for breakfast, cowboy*. We didn't think anything of it when the lightning seemed to reverse and change color, erupting blood red from the ocean, and we didn't figure it was really happening when it thickened, constructed a wall of fire that hissed and crackled and made the ocean boil. We dropped off to sleep gradually, lulled by the smoke, the warmth in our lungs, the electric air we breathed in and out.

I woke after what seemed like several hours of restless sleep, though it was hard to tell how much time had passed. Everything was dark, and my watch had stopped. My mouth was sticky, an intense thirst rising from the pit of my stomach and working its way up the folds of my esophagus. The temperature inside the car had soared, driven by our five bodies tossing and sweating all night, our blood heat. Flies and mosquitoes buzzed in my ears, a drone that rivaled the sound of the lightning. I'd dreamt about disaster: tsunamis, earthquakes, volcanic eruptions. I woke with the memory of ashes on my skin, lava dripping down my neck. When I opened my eyes, I saw flies. Buzzing through the cracked windows into Jen's long hair, lining the dashboard, knocking against the back window. My shirt was covered. When I brushed them off, exoskeletons crushed between my fingers.

Outside, either the pyrotechnic clouds had descended or something was burning. The air was thick with combustibility. I couldn't see the water, but I could hear it, the whisper I'd programmed onto my Soothing Sounds alarm clock at home. Just listening to it, my thirst intensified. I felt foggy, not quite lucid. I'd watched enough shipwreck movies to know that you weren't supposed to drink seawater, because it was salty and all that, but wouldn't it satisfy a little bit of my thirst? Wouldn't it clear my head?

Between the car and the ocean was a broad expanse of darkness, so dense that when I looked down, all I could see of my sandals was a faint outline. I tripped toward the sound of the water, stumbling over holes deep as booby traps from where, apparently, lightning had struck the beach. The moon was a gray smudge to my right, and remembering something about waves and lunar phases from a geology course, I turned toward it.

I never reached the ocean. Before I could get there, I slipped, coming down hard on something slick that gushed between my toes, then skimming across something soft, and finally, tumbling headlong into a slimy stretch of dead and dying fish. I imagined what I couldn't see, every foul, cold-blooded organism I'd ever seen behind glass or on a menu—mollusks, giant snails, sea snakes; kipper, lox, calamari. Creatures from old copies of *National Geographic*, that didn't belong in Florida waters, that hadn't yet been discovered. To my right, a puffer fish inflated to three times its size, needles extended, eyes stiff; to my left, a sting ray, tail still lashing. Everywhere, shellfish by the half ton, dolphin bodies rising like foothills, squid and salmon, the ridged underbelly of a whale. The pile writhed beneath me, full of severed gills and broken shells, a tangle of tentacles and antennae. Gills and blowholes straining, jaws that worked frantically and went slack.

It took three tries to push myself out of the mess, and even then it was with a mouthful of raw fish. Something stung my foot; something else bit into my arm. I shook myself free and gasped for air, scared. Nauseated. Below me, the wet, slapping sound of the depths. I was coated in their filth—delicacies, all, I thought in a moment of wry clarity—and covering this, a mist of burning sand.

I staggered backwards toward the dunes, or where I thought the dunes would be, my foot throbbing from where a barbed piece of stinger had gone through my sandal. I wiped myself with my shirt, fish guts under my fingernails, sand between my teeth. I dragged my foot up the side of the same dune we'd driven across two days ago, over the thorns and prickles of dehydrated plants, over splintered shells and broken bottles. I hardly felt the pain; I only wanted to get as far as I could from that wall of dead things.

The air was clearer up there, and I could see better. Some sort of dog or coyote watched me from farther up the dune, snarling, curling its lip to reveal wet teeth and, clamped between them, a dorsal fin. I couldn't remember whether I should run or play dead, but I was too tired to for either. Still growling, the dog wheeled around and headed toward the road. I bent to the ground, picked up a shard of glass, and threw it. Even after the dog had disappeared, I kept throwing things, screaming, raving, melodramatic as a made-for-TV movie. I threw anything in my reach: dead plants, sand, the flickering and fuming remains of what used to be the world.

I spent the night next to the road, desperate for a lone car— serial killers, rapists, bring on the Hitchhiker himself—anyone I could flag down and beg to take me away from there. All night, I waited. Flies and mosquitoes and lizards swarmed my legs, dove down my shirt, but I didn't move. *Dear God*, I thought, then didn't know how to continue. I started over: *Dear Hollywood. Give me a happy ending.* Then I laughed. I laughed until my stomach cramped, until the muscles in my abdomen twitched, wore out, and then finally stilled.

Jen woke me up hours later, crying, saying she'd thought I died or disappeared, and that if I'd died, maybe she would, too. She was so hysterical that I felt calm in comparison.

We climbed back over the dunes. The sun had risen into a dim spot in a mass of clouds that turned the beach gray. The tide had left behind an accumulation of fish and seaweed-entangled trash. Farther down the beach, we spotted a human-like object rocking in the shallows, but we neither investigated nor mentioned it again. The ocean it floated in was burgundy. There was a stench of rotting fish, but worse, a fumy smell, like plastic cups melting in a fire. Poisonous.

We covered our faces. We ran for the car.

Inside, we huddled around each other. Jen's face was swollen, and her hair was snarled. She still wore her bikini, but there were mean-looking lines where it'd rubbed into her shoulders and hips. Instead of speaking, she sniffled once in a while, and breathed deep, shuddering sighs as if to soothe herself. Zippy had his arm around her, but he didn't look much healthier. His dreadlocks had matted into one long lattice of hair. The burns on the backs of his legs had started to ooze.

"Listen to Jen, man," he said. "She doesn't sound good."

Jen sighed again, choked, put her head between her knees. "I'm thirsty," she whispered.

"We've got Diet Coke," Steve said. "That's it." He was the palest of the five of us and had fared the worst, physically. From his forehead to his toes, he was a bright crimson. He winced every time someone shifted on the towels. His nose was a bulbous, gleaming sore. His lips had swelled and split. When he talked, he tried not to move his face.

Charlie, on the other hand, had tanned to a nice bronze, and his hair was tousled in a stylized way. Give him a flag, and he could've been a Tommy Hilfiger spokesman. But mentally, he was as bad off as Jen. Rubbing the inch-long growth that'd sprouted on his cheeks, he kept saying, "What to do, what to do."

"I know what you can do," I said, massaging my swollen foot. "You can start walking. Find help. It could be days before anyone finds us."

My back itched something fierce, but when I reached around to scratch it, I felt nothing. Zippy reached over and pulled a long piece of dead skin from my shoulder. He handed it to me.

"Shit," I said. "Or we could sit here peeling our skin until there's nothing left."

Jen moaned.

"Where am I supposed to go?" Charlie said. He stopped rubbing his beard and stared at me with red-rimmed eyes. "I don't know where to go."

"Somebody has to help him," Jen said.

"Not me," Zippy said.

"I can't move," Steve said.

Five bedraggled faces gave me pleading looks. "I'll go," I said. "But I get the last Diet Coke."

We hiked back to the road, Charlie following me like a chained animal. He wore his shirt wrapped around his head. The temperature felt even hotter than it had yesterday, if that was possible. Oak trees with dead leaves lined the far side of the road, eking out a margin of shade, but between us and them was an expanse of syrupy asphalt. I tested it with a stick, which stuck to the surface. When I tried to pull it back out, the stick snapped in two. There were tracks where an animal had tried to cross, gotten stuck, and somehow fought its way back out.

"Looks like a dog," Charlie said, kneeling to look closely at the prints. "Maybe we're near a house."

That perked him up. He took the lead, picked up the pace. We tramped single file through dry grass and brambles, the sun at our backs. I was hoping for a gas station—fountain drinks, refrigerator cases with frosted glass, water so cold it formed a skin of ice on the surface.

"What I'd give for an Icee," I said, licking my lips and tasting salt. "Remember ice?"

"Don't think about it," Charlie said.

"Ice cubes, crushed ice, dry ice. Remember dry ice, Charlie?"

"Ice cream," he said. "That's what I want."

"Ice sculptures. Iced tea. Shoot, there was a whole Ice Age."

Charlie deliberately stepped on a lizard. "Can't think about it now," he said.

Across the road, the oak trees gave way to palms, their browning fronds pointing in every direction. We crossed a bridge at one point, the steel grids somehow cooler than the asphalt. Beneath us in the shallow water, nothing moved.

As soon as we stepped off the bridge, we saw it. The top half of a sign that just cleared the trees. ExxonMobil. Red, white, and blue.

"That's what I like to see," Charlie yelled.

"We're saved," I said, but the words sounded phony, the echo of someone I couldn't name.

We tripped over loose stones, tore through bushes, kicked up ant piles. We ran until we were breathless and hoarse, shipwrecked sailors spotting the rescue plane, lost hikers finding the trail, trapped miners taking hold of the lifeline. The Exxon sign was a beacon, our North Star. I thought of Gilligan, Dorothy, Ulysses. I shouted, "Land ho!"

We smelled the gas before we reached the station. The building was intact, but the windows were shattered and the parking lot was a slow-moving river, pocked with gas fires. The nozzles had fallen from their holders and were half-sunk in asphalt. We shouted, screamed, but only a dog appeared in the doorway— lighter than the one I'd seen last night, almost blindingly white, except for a red stain around its muzzle.

We couldn't go any farther because a few feet ahead, the road had spilled over the curb. Big bubbles rose from the blacktop, spraying us when they burst. Charlie stepped in a pile of fire ants, and we wasted several minutes wiping his legs down. For the first time, I noticed the lack of birds—not even a seagull. Not even a vulture. Perhaps as we'd been heading south, cruising at a cool eighty miles per hour, jamming to retro rock and eating pork rinds, all the birds were flying north for the summer.

On the way back, I saw three lizards stuck in tar, like miniature replicas of the La Brea pits. Others raced through the underbrush and poked their heads out of tunnels in the sand. They seemed to be getting along just famously. Whenever I got a clear shot, I stepped on them.

We were gone less than an hour. By the time we returned, the sky was packed with ultra-white clouds. Zippy hung halfway out the driver's seat of the Suburban when he saw us marching down the dune. "Did you find something?" he shouted.

I shook my head. Zippy's hair was a dark blot among an all-encompassing glare. I didn't think anything could be brighter until lightning flashed again over the water, atomic in intensity.

"Storm's brewing," Charlie said.

"A hot one," I said.

We didn't tell the rest of them about the gas station, the dog. We offered the damaged road as an excuse. Everyone agreed that we shouldn't have gone, that it was better not to split up. That the National Guard must be out by now, and the Red Cross and the Salvation Army. That if we listened carefully, we might be able to hear the sirens already.

Charlie and I piled into the back, relieved, at last, to be out of the sun. I split the last Coke with Jen. Her lips were white. She said mine were, too. Steve dozed in the passenger's seat. Zippy sat on the cooler lid behind the steering wheel, looking sick.

The caffeine made Jen giddy, and for a few minutes she acted like her old self again. She tucked her hair into a bun, tickled Zippy, smoothed Charlie's hair.

"So, what are we going to eat," she said, like one of us might have an answer.

"Sushi," Zippy said, pointing at the rotting carcasses on the beach. I thought of the dogs, wondered how long it would be before we were fighting them for meals.

"We could eat each other, like in those *Reader's Digest* stories," Jen said, giggling. "I vote Liz." She tapped my arm. "She's well-done."

"Do you think it would be bad," Zippy said, still looking at the fish. "To eat that? I mean, isn't it better than starvation?"

"That's disgusting, Zippy," Jen said. "I'd rather eat Liz."

"I'm sick of this," Steve said. "Shut up and let me sleep."

"Me, too," Charlie said. "I think I've got heat exhaustion. I could pass out right now."

"Heat exhaustion," Jen said, giggling. "Who doesn't have heat exhaustion?"

I was beat from the walk, too, and even in the brightness my eyes were already closing. Jen was the last one conscious I saw before dozing off. She stared out the front windshield, grinning maniacally, her teeth reflecting the electric glow.

We woke to more thunder, but this time it seemed promising. It was louder, closer, heavier. We didn't dare say it, but I could tell by the desperation in my friends' faces that we were all thinking it: *rain*. We would've taken anything that was either wet or edible. Snow, hail, sleet; acid rain, yellow rain, freezing rain; a deluge, a tempest, a monsoon. We watched more clouds roll in from the south. Charlie tumbled out, and the rest of us followed, climbing onto the hood and roof. "There it is," he said. Down the beach, still far into the distance, gleaming in the brilliant light: a torrential downpour. A beautiful, vigorous rain storm.

"Oh, god," Zippy said. "Thank you, god."

"We need something to catch the water," I said, digging out the cooler. Steve set beer bottles in the sand, and we emptied the ash tray, Jen's shampoo bottle, and Charlie's mouthwash. We hugged each other, high-fived, stated the obvious: "This ought to cool things off." We began to talk about the heat as if it had already passed. "That was weird," Charlie said. "For a while there, I was really scared."

I watched the rain wall, flickering like a curtain of tiny candles. "Will you look at that," I said. "I've never seen rain glitter like that."

As I spoke, a delicate mist reached us. Not cold, exactly, but perceptibly moist. "It's here," I said, unable to hold back. Then, "Ouch," as I felt a prick on my arm.

"Shit," Charlie said from the roof. "Damn bugs."

"You get stung?" Steve said. He was perched on the hood next to me, his red legs dangling over the edge. He held my arm close to his face. "We should get back in the car," he said.

I surveyed my arm. There, where there should have been a swelling bug bite, was a burn blister. Round, as if from a spark.

"Right now," Steve said, and at the same time, Zippy said, "I don't think this is from a mosquito." Steve grabbed my arm, and electricity shot between us.

What followed was impossible. We piled into the car and rolled the windows up just as the first few drops hit the windshield. They sparked as they rolled beneath the hood and into the engine. The bigger drops stuck, hovering on the glass. Inside each was a tiny white light, a miniature star, its lightning bolt arms reaching out to the perimeters of the droplet. Steam rose from the car, and from the dead animals on the beach.

"It's so pretty," Jen said sadly. "I wish we had a camera."

"It's still rain," Charlie said. "Even this mutant shit. It might at least cool things off."

It rained all night and into the morning—hot, galvanized, wet. It was as if the lightning from the previous nights had shattered into liquid fire and, true to form, anywhere a puddle gathered on the beach, a fire sprouted. Our hair stood on end, the Diet Coke cans stuck together. The cooler outside melted into the sand. Rain thundered onto the roof of the car, every drop exploding like a rocket.

The water pooled quickly, the dead animals acting like a levee, and it soaked the beach and trickled inland, pockets of flame leaping upward like oil fires. The sudden humidity caused the windows to fog up, but even without Zippy's frenzied struggle to clear them with the hem of his shirt, we knew the water was rising. We could feel its heat advancing toward the car.

Inside, we were pulling on all of our clothes. Swimsuits, tank tops, T-shirts, jeans. We tied shirts around our feet, ripped pieces of flooring to wrap around our hands. We tucked away hair, zipped duffle bags around our heads. We urinated on ourselves, sent up prayers, made tasteless jokes. We waited until the first sparks trickled in through the air conditioner vents. They dropped to the floor, and Steve stomped them out. Charlie opened the door.

"Go," I said.

The rain lit a path to the dune. My muscles revved, woke from days of sitting still. For the first time since we'd arrived, I felt the familiar sensation under all the clothes of my body beginning to sweat. The rain burned holes in our clothes quickly, sunk straight through to the skin, and then through that, too. But for a few minutes, there on the beach as the world ended, it felt good just to run.

Katherine Anne Porter Prize in Short Fiction

The Katherine Anne Porter Prize in Short Fiction is awarded annually to a collection of publishable length consisting of a combination of short-shorts, short stories, or a novella. Selection is made by an eminent writer. The contest is partially sponsored by the University of North Texas English Department. Barbara Rodman, associate professor of English at UNT, serves as series editor. The winner receives $1,000 and publication by the University of North Texas Press.